2099

traitor

P9-CQW-107

BOOK 3

2099

traitor

John Peel

BOOK 3

AN
APPLE
PAPERBACK

SCHOLASTIC INC.
New York Toronto London Auckland Sydney
Mexico City New Delhi Hong Kong

This is for Andrew, Veronica, Katie, and Sam

ISBN 0-439-06032-X

12 11 10 9 8 7 6 5 4 3 2 1   0 1 2 3 4 5 6/0

Printed in the U.S.A.

First Scholastic printing, January 2000

Prologue

Tristan stared in horror at Inspector Shimoda and her partner. He could do nothing as the shield placed the restraints on his wrists and ankles. They didn't look like old-fashioned shackles, more like bracelets, but they acted the same way. If he tried to escape or to attack the inspector, the computer chips inside the restraints would draw his hands and ankles together instantly, tripping and felling him. As the restraints went on, Tristan felt absolutely helpless and humiliated.

The stupid shield wouldn't even listen to him! "I'm not the person you want," he tried to explain again.

Shimoda smiled grimly. "Believe me, Connor, you *are*

the person I want. After what you did to New York, I've been after no one else. And I am really, really glad I caught you. Even if I did have to chase you into space to make my arrest."

Tristan looked around the room, which the other police officer was in the process of electronically sealing. It was on the space station Overlook, thousands of miles above the surface of Earth. This was the birthplace of the Doomsday Virus, which had nearly destroyed the great city of New York. It had also resulted in the deaths of so many people that the final count hadn't even been made yet.

"But these aren't my rooms," Tristan protested. "They belong to a boy named Devon. I tracked him down here and came up to stop the Doomsday Virus that he created."

The other shield looked up and snorted. "According to cell analysis," she commented, holding up her portalab, "the only genetic material in here before we arrived was yours. These are your rooms, all right."

"*Listen* to me," Tristan begged. "That's not *my* genetic material — it's Devon's. One of us is the clone of the other, which is why it looks just like mine. He claims I'm the clone, but I don't know if that's true or not. He tends to lie a lot."

Shimoda sighed. "Look, Connor, we know you're

making up this fairy tale about having a clone because you know somebody made one of Dennis Borden. It's obvious that you think you can try and confuse us by claiming there's a clone of you, too. But it won't work. Human cloning is illegal, and would only be done under the most desperate of circumstances. Cloning a man like Borden — who is very important — might be worth taking such a risk. Cloning a nobody like you . . . well, it wouldn't be very smart."

"I don't know if it's smart or not," Tristan protested. "But it's been done. I've seen this clone of mine, and he's totally evil."

"Okay," the second shield said. "If this clone of yours exists, where is he? Why doesn't he show up on the Net? And why does nobody else know about him?"

"I don't know where he is," Tristan admitted. "I had hoped he'd be here when I arrived, but he's fled. He doesn't show up on the Net because he's a brilliant hacker. Plus, he's being protected by some weird group named Quietus."

Shimoda looked elated. "So you know about Quietus?" she asked.

"Only a little," Tristan said. "It's a group of crooks who have a grand plan of some kind. Maybe to rule the world, I don't really know. Devon works for them. They need him. And they're the people who've been trying to kidnap me. You know about that, because you stopped them from getting me."

Shimoda shook her head. "I'm certain that was just one of your tricks. You wanted to throw me off your scent, so you staged a fake kidnapping. It almost worked, because I *did* think you might be innocent. But there's just too much proof that you're guilty for me to accept that any longer."

"The men who tried to kidnap me tried again a short while ago," Tristan informed her. "Only the release of the virus stopped them."

"Is that why you released it?" the other shield asked. "To stop them?"

"I *didn't* release it!" Tristan protested, even though he sensed it wouldn't do him any good. "Devon did. It broke down their flitter and killed them."

"But *you* just happened to get away?" The woman shook her head. "Why would Devon kill his own men if he already had you, like he wanted? Connor, your story isn't making any sense."

"It's not making sense simply because I don't know all the information," Tristan said. He could tell that these two shields weren't believing his story. They'd made up their minds already, and nothing he was saying would get through to them. The only thing he could do, he realized, was to go along with them for now and hope that he could convince the courts he was innocent when he was put on trial.

If he ever got to trial. Because even if the shields didn't believe that Devon existed, Tristan knew that he did. And Devon and Quietus wouldn't want Tristan publically exposed and talking about them.

He'd be lucky if he lived long enough to get back to Earth. . . .

1

aki Shimoda took one last look around the suite of rooms that Tristan had occupied on Overlook, and then nodded to Lt. Jill Barnes, her temporary partner. "Okay, I think we can seal it up for now," she decided. They would have to go over it again later, since they simply didn't have the time and the resources for a full analysis right now. Besides, the room's Terminal had been totally wiped of information, beyond any kind of reconstruction. Naturally, Tristan claimed it had been the work of this mythical clone of his, Devon, but it had to be his own handiwork. He'd been able to control this place from Earth without much problem, thanks to the

Net. But when the Doomsday Virus had broken down the New York Net, he'd been forced to come here in person to deactivate all of his equipment and cover his tracks. When he realized he couldn't get away, he'd contrived to destroy his virus and then make up the story of a clone in order to get away with what he had done.

It was typical of a criminal like Tristan to do that. He clearly thought he was a lot smarter than the shields because he'd managed to create a killer virus and release it. No doubt he got some sort of a kick out of believing he was so much better and smarter than "normal" human beings, and then inflicting pain and suffering on them. And he was egotistical enough to think he could get away with it all, pretending to have saved everyone by destroying his own virus! The boy was clearly sick. She didn't know whether he needed treatment or just locking up for the rest of his natural — or unnatural — life. That wasn't her decision to make; it was up to the judge. Her job was simply to stop him from harming anyone else, and to bring him in.

Of course, that might prove to be easier said than done. In one respect at least, Tristan was telling the truth. This criminal organization named Quietus was very mysterious and very efficient. She'd already realized that the group had at least one agent inside the shield force. She could no longer trust almost anyone, until she could uncover the traitor in their ranks. That was why she'd called in Lt. Barnes for help; she was from outside Shimoda's group, and Shimoda knew the woman was honest and trustworthy. She wasn't sure who else she could say this about.

She wasn't even certain of her own boss, Peter Chen. Chen was head of internal security for Computer Control, a very important man. If Quietus needed an agent in the shields, then he'd be the perfect person. Shimoda had already discovered that Chen had apparently made some really stupid "mistakes" that nobody should ever make, mistakes that conveniently helped Tristan and Quietus. And he had known all about Genia, even though Shimoda hadn't reported on her to him.

At the thought of the young girl, the inspector had another twinge of conscience. Genia was a thief, true, and didn't play by the rules. But she had helped in tracking down Tristan and the virus. Plus, she'd grown up in the Underworld, abandoned by her parents and neglected by society at large. You couldn't expect her to have a normal conscience with a background like that. And Genia had come to Shimoda for help, which the inspector had promised her. But Chen, somehow, knew about Genia, and had ordered the girl arrested, tried, and sentenced to Ice for years. Shimoda had fought against this decision, but lost.

Chen, obviously, was trying to handicap her work. Which was why she hadn't yet mentioned to him that she had gone to arrest Tristan. She wanted to have the boy in the justice system before she told her boss the truth. Once Tristan was being processed and in the public eye, even Chen couldn't free the culprit. Until then, Shimoda wanted to keep everything secret.

She had a shield Ramjet at the docking port of Overlook, and she and Barnes could take Tristan back to Earth in that. Once they were safe in Jersey City, Tristan would be booked and charged and tried. *Then* she'd tell Chen all about it. It hardly mattered if he was furious by then — she would have done her job, and he could hardly punish her for it. Or free Tristan. She just needed a little more time.

But time was the one thing she wouldn't get.

Barnes finished sealing the room, setting up a force field that could only be opened with the correct coding. Only Barnes and Shimoda knew what that was, so no agent of Tristan or Quietus could get in and steal whatever evidence there might be.

Shimoda's wrist-comp beeped, and she winced. She could hardly refuse to take the message, since it was from shield headquarters. But when she answered it, Chen would know where she was. Barnes looked at her, and Shimoda knew she was finally out of luck. She tapped the ACCEPT key and the screen lit up. It was, as she'd expected and feared, her boss.

"Shimoda!" he snapped. "I just discovered that you requisitioned a Ramjet and failed to file a flight plan for it. Now I find you're on Overlook! You'd better have a really good explanation for this, or else I'm going to charge you with dereliction of duty."

Shimoda flushed in anger but kept her temper. "I do have a good explanation," she replied. She wasn't going to call him *sir*. "I have caught Tristan Connor red-handed. The virus has been destroyed, and the Net should be free again now."

"What?" Chen blinked and then moved out of vision, obviously checking what she had just said. Then he reappeared, looking stunned. "You're right — the virus has gone entirely from the Net. But . . . why didn't you report this? Why are you not observing the rules?"

"Surely that's obvious?" she asked. "Haven't you noticed by now that there is a traitor within the shield ranks? Someone in our department is working for Quietus and Tristan Connor instead of for us. I knew that if I had requested the Ramjet through official channels, the traitor would have discovered this and warned Tristan."

"That makes sense, I imagine," Chen said tightly. "But could you not, at least, have trusted me?"

Shimoda stared back coldly at his image. "No. I could not."

He would've had to be stupid to miss her point, and he wouldn't have risen to be the head of security if he was stupid. "You think *I'm* the traitor?" he asked her quietly.

"You *are* the logical suspect," she informed him.

"I see." His lips tightened. "And have you reported this suspicion of yours to anyone?"

"Not yet. It's in my comp files, though. If anything happens to me, all of the evidence and suspicions I have will be sent directly to Van Dreelen. He is, after all, *your* boss. And I'm sure he'll act on what I say if I happen to die a suspicious death."

"I'm sure he'd pay it a great deal of attention," Chen agreed dryly. "And I imagine my assurances that I am *not* a traitor will not influence you in the slightest?"

"Hardly," Shimoda admitted.

"Then may I ask what you intend to do now?"

Shimoda had been dreading this, but she couldn't lie. Chen knew where she was, and had to know the tracking codes from her Implant Chip and the Ramjet. He could track her even if she lied. "I'm returning to shield HQ with my prisoner," she informed him. "I expect him to then be placed directly into the legal system and tried immediately."

"I'll start the arrangements now," Chen promised. "The judge and trial crew will be awaiting his arrival. Is Connor prepared to admit his guilt?"

"No. He . . . claims that a clone of him exists and has been doing everything that we know Connor has done."

"Then he'll need to be given Truzac and forced to confess. I'll see to it." He moved to cut the link.

"Mr. Chen," Shimoda said calmly. "You are the only person who knows where I am and why. Tell nobody else. At the moment, I only *believe* that you are the traitor in our ranks. If anything should happen to me as I return to Earth, it will clearly be because of your interference. In that case, I shall *know* you are the traitor, and act accordingly. I trust I make myself clear?"

"Perfectly clear, Inspector," he answered. "I have absolutely no problem understanding what you are saying. And if I *were* guilty, I'd have to be insane to try and stop you, wouldn't I?"

"Yes," Shimoda agreed. "So I shall have to hope you

are quite sane, shalln't I?" She cut the link and sighed heavily.

Tristan stared at her. His dark, curly hair needed brushing, but his piercing eyes were bright. "You think your boss works for Quietus?" he asked.

"You should know," she snapped. "I hope they ask you about that when they get you on Truzac."

"What's Truzac?" he asked.

"A truth drug. It's how trials are conducted. You're given a shot of it and you're forced to tell the truth."

"Really?" He actually looked relieved. "They'll give me this stuff and I'll have to be honest?"

"Yes."

"Wonderful." He smiled. "Because I'll tell them what I told you. Then they'll *know* I'm telling the truth, and they'll let me go. Then you can go after the *real* criminal."

Shimoda felt a pang of uncertainty. Tristan had cheered up since she'd mentioned Truzac. Was it just possible that he actually was telling the truth?

Or, more likely, was it possible that Quietus had figured out some way of beating Truzac? That was theoretically impossible, of course. But so was destroying New York by shutting down the Net, and Tristan had done that. Was it too far-fetched to assume that some way of blocking Truzac might be found? And, if so, did this mean that Tristan might literally be able to get away with murder? If they questioned him under Truzac and he stuck to his story, the judge might *have* to release him.

How could she allow that to happen? Shimoda was certain that Tristan was the villain; the idea that he might have some method of escaping justice made her sick. Obviously, she would have to have a good, long think about this.

She gestured, and Tristan started walking down the corridor, toward the docking area. Shimoda and Barnes fell in behind him. They had their weapons holstered, since Tristan didn't seem to be planning an escape, but Shimoda was constantly scanning all around them. There might well be other Quietus agents on the station, and if they knew about the arrest there might be serious trouble. She wished she could carry her tazer, but she wasn't allowed to except in emergencies. People didn't like to see guns these days, and they might get nervous if she had hers out.

The second she saw anything suspicious, though, she'd draw. And she could see the same determination on Barnes's face. The other shield was just as tense, and her eyes flickered all around as they walked.

Crossing the shopping area was a nightmare. There were so many people here — dozens of them. Shimoda was used to Earth, where crowds of four people were as many as you normally got. Here, though, the people seemed to *like* being close to one another, and enjoyed shopping in real places instead of at .comstores. It seemed strange and almost sick to her. But then, she supposed it took a special sort of person to live anywhere off Earth. It wasn't something she'd ever want to do.

Somehow, they made it across without incident, though it strained her nerves. Tristan was red-faced, obviously ashamed. The passersby, of course, realized that he was a prisoner, though they could hardly imagine why. He was only a teenager, and there was probably a lot of speculation as to why two shields from Earth had come all this way to arrest him instead of having station security do the job. Well, let them talk. And Tristan *should* be ashamed.

The docking port was on the outskirts of the station. Gravity was less here, as it was caused by the spin of Overlook. Farther out to the rim of the station, the floors moved slower, so the feel of gravity was less. They had to walk slower to avoid bouncing off the walls or ceiling. It took some getting used to, but Shimoda didn't have the time. She led the way to the waiting Ramjet, and then fastened Tristan firmly into the prisoner compartment. He said nothing, but looked haunted. Maybe he was finally having an attack of conscience, but Shimoda was sure it was simply that he realized he was going to be in serious trouble very soon. He'd always imagined he'd get away with everything, thinking he was so much better than everyone else. Now he had discovered the truth.

"It won't be long till we're back on Earth," she promised him. "And then you'll be going on Ice for the rest of your miserable life."

"I don't think so," he told her. "If Quietus knows I'm on my way down, they'll try and finish what they started earlier. They'll try to kill me." He shook his head. "I really hope you're as good as you think you are. I'll bet you that we're attacked on the way back. Then you'll know I'm telling the truth."

"You wouldn't know the truth if it bit you on your ankles," Barnes snapped. She closed the holding cell door on him.

Shimoda went back to the pilot's compartment. The shield pilot was waiting for them to strap themselves in. As soon as they did, he began the undocking process. Shimoda lay back and closed her eyes. The first stage was over: She had her prisoner. Now they had to survive the second, and get him back to Earth. Though she didn't agree with much that the boy said, she had to agree with him on one point:

It was very unlikely that they'd be allowed to journey home safely.

2

enia stared across the short space separating her from the newcomer. Her mind felt numb. She had believed she was incapable of any further shocks. After all, she'd been attacked, narrowly escaped being killed by the supposedly nonexistent monster called the Tabat, teamed up with the police, and then was tried as a thief and sentenced to Ice. And all within the past couple of days. She'd seen her life as a successful crook be finished forever, and watched New York City burn. And now . . .

"I'm your father," the man said gently. He looked almost on the verge of tears.

Her *father*? All she knew about her father was what she'd heard from her mother before she'd died and left Genia alone in the Underworld as a child. Her mother had simply told her that her father had been a businessman who'd tried embezzling funds when he couldn't make ends meet any other way. And he'd been stupid enough at it to get caught and sent to jail. As a result of his criminal actions, Genia's mother had been stripped of everything and forced to live in the Underworld, where Genia was born.

Her *father*? The jerk responsible for everything that had ever happened to her? Genia kept her face impassive; she *never* gave anything away if she could avoid it. She examined his face, and realized that he was almost overflowing with emotion. A sudden determination filled her.

"Poppa?" she asked, making her voice tremble slightly. "Is it really you?"

"My little girl," he said, and this time he did sob. It was pathetic. He moved forward and threw his arms around her, hugging her tightly. Genia forced herself to hug him back, though she'd much rather have spat in his face. It was bad enough that he had let her down all her life; what was worse was that he'd gotten caught. It showed how useless he was, even as a criminal. Then again, she'd been caught, too, but only because she'd been betrayed by that lying shield, Shimoda. Genia knew she'd been even dumber than her father, trusting the promise of a police officer!

Her father looked older than she'd pictured. She'd always thought of him somehow as a neat, dark-haired man of about thirty. He was actually a gray-haired man running slightly to plump who looked almost twice that age. Maybe being here in Ice had done that to him. It was hard to forget that they were all trapped here, underground, with the raging winter of Antarctica above them. The only way in or out was by a shield jet, so even if somebody could escape, it would only be to their deaths in the ice and freezing winds. Living with the knowledge of no escape might age anyone.

Finally, her father had gotten his fill of hugging and sobbing. He held her at arm's length and stared at her. "You've become a young lady," he said, almost proudly.

Genia wanted to throw up. Couldn't he think of something more original than that? "I guess," she said instead, in her best little-girl voice. "It wasn't easy, Poppa. I was all alone." She even managed to produce a small tear to trickle down her cheek, and she felt rather proud of that. She could see that he was buying every fake emotion she could pump at him. He really must at least *think* he cared about her. Amazing!

And very, very useful.

"I'm sorry I couldn't have been with you," he said, his voice almost breaking. "But I've been condemned to Ice for life."

"Like father, like daughter," a cynical voice suggested. Genia had forgotten about the woman who was supposed to be showing her where she would live, eat, and exist on Ice. She cast the woman a frosty glower, which didn't affect her in the slightest.

"It's all my fault you're here," her father sobbed, hugging Genia again.

Yes, it is, she thought to herself. "Don't blame yourself, Poppa," she said aloud. "You couldn't help me. I was forced to live all alone. I don't know how I managed it, but I did. And we're together again now."

"Yes," he gasped, tears running down his cheeks. "Yes, we are. But what a place to be together in." He wiped at his cheeks with the back of one hand. "I dreamed of meeting you for so many, many years. I thought I would never see you."

"I didn't even know if you were still alive, Poppa," Genia whispered.

"Well, you know it now." He hugged her again.

Genia was starting to get tired of this. Maybe she should have just spat in his face, after all? But she was new here, and she needed protection and help. He was the best possible choice, at least for the moment. He'd survived sixteen years here. Maybe he was a jerk, but he could at least help her. And with all the emotion and guilt she was piling on him right now, he *would* help her. He'd do anything she wanted. . . .

She pretended to wipe at her own tears, and managed to snuffle a little. "I guess . . . I guess I'd better get to my cell."

Her father nodded. "They give you a few clothes," he told her. "I can get you more, because those aren't very comfortable. At least, so I'm told."

Genia realized that his clothing wasn't the standard jumpsuit, but looked a lot more expensive. "You can do that?" she asked in a small, childlike voice.

He shrugged. "I'm . . . valuable here," he told her, with a slight smile. "I can get things that are needed. And for my girl, I'll do whatever I can."

Perfect! Genia smiled, genuinely this time. "That's wonderful, Poppa."

"For my girl? What else could I do?" He looked at the female convict. "Sarai here will take you to your cell and show you what's what. I'll see about getting you some better clothes. Is there anything else you need right now? Makeup? Do you wear makeup?" He looked anxiously at her.

It was all she could do not to roll her eyes. "No, Poppa," she answered. "I . . . I don't feel right doing that. I'm still kind of . . ." She couldn't say *young,* but she could leave him with that impression. Let him picture her as his darling little baby girl. It would make getting things from him so much easier.

"That's okay." He stroked her cheek. "Off you go. I'll see you soon. It is *so* good to see you finally, my dear, sweet baby."

"You too, Poppa." She let him hug her again, and then followed meekly behind Sarai to the women's wing of the prison. When the door closed behind them, Sarai gave her a skeptical glance. "That was some performance," she said dryly. "But you don't fool me."

Genia snorted. "I don't *have* to fool you. So what are you going to do? Tell *Poppa* that I'm a wicked, ungrateful girl and he should put me over his knee and spank me?"

"Quite an attitude you've got, too," Sarai mused. Then she shook her head. "No, I'm not stupid enough to try and make Marten see the truth. Right now, you're pretending to be exactly what he's been wishing and praying sixteen years for. More fool, him. He'll find out the truth eventually. And so will you."

"What will I find out?" Genia asked.

"That you're stuck here with him forever, and anything you do wrong now will come back and haunt you later. They tell you your sentence is just a few years, but that's not true. You can only get out of here if you feel sorry for what you've done. And if you were capable of feeling sorry for it, you wouldn't have been sent here in the first place." Sarai smiled nastily. "We're examples to the rest of the world, you see. If they want to know what happens if you decide to be a crook, they point people here. We're on Ice forever as bad examples."

"I am *not* stuck here!" snarled Genia. "I'm getting out of here just as soon as I can."

"Dream on." Sarai laughed. "Everybody says that when they first arrive. And then they wise up and realize that there's no way out of here."

"There's a way in," Genia said stubbornly. "That means there's a way out. It just takes brains to discover it."

"You think you're that much smarter than us, then?" mocked Sarai. "That you can find a way to escape from Ice, even though it's never been done before?"

"That's what makes it so much fun. I specialize in doing what has never been done before. And, yes. I think I'm a whole lot smarter than you."

"Well, you're certainly not strong on humility." Sarai gestured at an open door. "Here's your place, young lady. Sorry, there's no room service." She led the way in. "It used to be my cell."

Genia looked around. It wasn't actually as bad as

she'd feared — the door didn't have bars, and there was a separate bathroom, so she had some privacy, at least. Aside from that, there was a small bed, a table and chair, and a small wardrobe. "Wallowing in nostalgia?" she asked Sarai. "Or is it muck?" She ran a finger across the chair back, and it came away dusty.

"You want it clean, you clean it," Sarai said. "Make of it what you will."

"Isn't there a lock?" Genia asked.

"No."

"There will be," Genia vowed. "As long as I'm here, I'll want some privacy."

"Trust me," Sarai said sourly, "nobody's going to want to be your buddy. Except your father, and he'll soon learn. Until your attitude improves, you certainly won't need a lock, because nobody will want to come near you."

Genia scowled at the woman. "You said this used to be your cell. What happened? You get moved to the penthouse, or something?"

Sarai stared coldly at her. "Your father and I were married ten years ago. We share the same cell now."

"Wow, he didn't waste time, did he? Abandon one wife, take another." Genia smiled, very insincerely. "Oh, should I be calling you *Momma* now?"

"Try it and I'll slap you silly." Sarai glared at her. "I

don't like you. I almost wish you *could* escape, because I know you're going to break Marten's heart. But it's not possible. Besides, what have you got to go back to? You were on the streets of the Underworld, not in high society. This place is better than that."

Genia snorted. "Maybe you'd be living in squalor in the Underworld," she boasted. "But I wasn't, not by a long shot. I have my own apartment, computers, toys, clothes, books — anything I wanted, I simply took. I told you, I do what others consider impossible. I lived better in the Underworld than many *respectable* citizens in New York."

"So you'll be going back there, hey?" asked Sarai. "Back to your fancy lifestyle and all those lovely possessions? That's why you want out of here?" She shrugged. "That might have appealed to me, too, at one time. But not anymore."

"That's not why I'm going back," Genia answered. "I'm going back for revenge."

"Revenge?" Sarai hooted with amusement. "Well, doesn't that take all? And who do you aim to get revenge on, child?"

"Everyone who ever betrayed me," Genia answered, anger rising inside her. "Starting with the shield who promised to protect me and who turned me over to the system. And then on the system itself." She smiled sweetly. "And on you if you try messing with me. *Nobody* walks all over me and gets away with it. Nobody messes with me and gets to boast of it. They will pay, all of them."

Sarai raised her eyebrows in mock surprise. "Well, *now* you sound like your daddy's long-lost little girl! You've been punished, so you want your revenge! What a brat you are." She pointed at Genia. "You were caught red-handed, you little rat, and sent here because this is where you belong. You'll never get out of here, and if you're only looking for revenge, you'll never get it. Emotions like that can burn you up and consume you here, child. Give them up. The sooner you do, the sooner you'll be able to get on with your life."

"I *will* get on with my life," Genia promised. "Only it won't be here, that much I can tell you."

Sarai shook her head in sorrow. "Forget about it, kid. It won't work." Then she sighed. "But I know you'll ignore my advice, so why do I even bother? Welcome to Ice, kid. Get used to it." Turning her back, she marched out of the room.

Furiously, Genia threw herself onto the bed. She wanted to cry with rage and frustration, but she wouldn't allow herself to let go. Nobody here would ever see her cry. She didn't care what Sarai thought, she *would* escape. The losers who had tried before were just not smart enough to make it, that was all. There was a way out of here, and she'd find it.

Then she would show Inspector Shimoda what betrayal really meant. . . .

After a while, she had calmed down enough to be in control of her emotions again. It was time to start looking for ways out of here. She checked the room thoroughly for anything that might help, but there wasn't much. There were two other jumpsuits in the closet, and a couple of pairs of faded underwear that had probably belonged to some other prisoner. She had no intentions of wearing hand-me-downs. There was an extra pair of the slippers she wore, and nothing else. In the bathroom, there was toothpaste, hair gel, body soap, two towels, and a spare roll of toilet paper.

Nothing that inspired her with thoughts of a plan to escape.

There was a knock at the door, and her father peered in. "It's not much, I know," he apologized. "I've brought you some things."

"Thank you, Poppa," she said. She was actually almost grateful to him. He'd brought a comb and styles for her hair, a little food, a small screen, and some real clothes, including new underwear.

"I hope it's okay," he said. "I really don't know what girls your age wear, or anything. If you need something else, just ask me or Sarai."

"Sarai?" Genia snorted. "She doesn't like me, Poppa. I think she's jealous because you're paying attention to me. Maybe you should leave me and go be with her. After all, she's been with you ten years, and I haven't been with you at all." She managed to sniffle, and almost produced a tear.

"Nonsense!" her father exclaimed. "Sarai's a wonderful woman. She's just . . . Well, you have to realize that we don't exactly get the cream of society here. She's naturally suspicious of newcomers. I'm sure you'll both get along wonderfully once you've settled in here."

"I don't aim to settle in here, Poppa," she told him firmly. "I'm going to escape, just as soon as I figure out a plan. And I want you to come with me. I can look after us both, and you'll be very happy. Oh, and Sarai, too, I guess."

"Escape?" He looked confused. "Don't you realize that there's no escape? Besides, where would you escape *to*? Back to those horrible streets and slums of New York? Didn't you know it was almost destroyed these past few days?"

"Of course; I was there." Genia scowled. "How come you know? Do they let you watch vids here?"

"I have a desk-comp," he said casually. "I'm rather good at . . . getting things. It's what I do here. I manage to bring in things for the prisoners and the staff, so they tolerate me. I'm actually doing quite well here."

Genia was stunned. He was *proud* of what he had managed. He'd obviously built up a kind of a black market in this jail, and made some sort of a life for himself. And while he was doing it, he'd let his wife and daughter rot in the streets of the Underworld. And then, when his wife was dead, he'd married one of the other inmates here! It took every ounce of her self-restraint to keep from slapping his stupid face. She had to force herself to remember that, for the time being, she needed his help. She needed him to think that she was glad to see him, and grateful for everything he did for her.

Later, she'd pay *him* back, too.

"That's wonderful, Poppa," she said, forcing a smile onto her face. "Is there any chance you could get a comp for me, too? It's the only thing I really miss from my old life. I'd *love* to play games on one." She actually managed to produce a few tears this time, mostly because she had her fists firmly clenched, and was digging her nails into her palms so hard it *hurt*.

Her father smiled fondly. "I'll see what I can do," he promised. "Nothing is too much for my little girl." He tousled her hair. "Well, I'm sure you'll want to change out of those dreadful clothes, and maybe wash your hair, or whatever. Then it'll be dinnertime. And after that, you can come to my room and play on my comp for a while." He sighed happily. "Genia, you've no idea what today has meant to me."

"Oh, I think I have," she said, wide-eyed and innocent. "I've found my Poppa. . . ."

He hugged her again, and then left, still on the verge of tears. Genia closed the door and grimaced. It wasn't getting any easier, being nice to him. But if he could get her a comp, then she'd be one step closer to freeing herself. Once she had access to the Net, nothing could stop her.

Nothing!

3

It felt really strange being on the Moon. Devon couldn't keep a grin off his face as he half-walked, half-bounced down the corridors of Armstrong City, toward the suite of offices he had rented under a very fake name. One of the advantages of being a computer genius was that he could cover his traces without any problems whatsoever. He had no desire to be found right now by anyone — especially Quietus — and he had a lot of work to do. Even with all of the pressure on him, he was enjoying the bizarre sensation of walking in only one-sixth of normal Earth gravity. You tended to bounce rather than walk, and it felt funny.

Armstrong City was the largest on the Moon, with almost four thousand people living and working here. Naturally, it was mostly built under the surface and consisted of tunnels carved into lunar rocks that were very well-sealed against leaks. There was no air to speak of (or with!) on the lunar surface, so it was vitally important that the city be extremely airtight. Plus, since the "days" were two weeks long, the city had to be protected against the extreme cold of the lunar night and the extreme heat of the lunar day. Building it underground made that simpler. Plus, since the Moon had no atmosphere, it had no protection against solar radiation like Earth had from its ozone layer. Instead, the tons of rock over their heads took care of it.

Living permanently underground seemed strange to Devon — and it accounted for the Moon-dwellers' main nickname of "moles" — but he could hardly talk. After all, he'd lived his entire life until now on Outlook, in orbit above Earth. And he hadn't even realized it until he'd finally left his rooms. So spending some time underground on the Moon would hardly be a challenge for him.

He also found it kind of strange to have people around him. He'd seen lots of people in his life, of course, when he used Virtual Reality programs. But they had never actually been *there*. Now, as he walked through the corridors, he saw ten or twenty real-life people. Most, seeing his grin, smiled at him or greeted him politely. Devon enjoyed saying hello back to them. The poor jerks didn't have a clue who he was, which made it all funnier. If they had known, they might have thought him the most dangerous criminal in the solar system. That amused Devon most of all.

He'd have to start writing his autobiography. After all, there was no real point in being a brilliant criminal if everyone didn't appreciate your genius. Of course, right now he had to keep a low profile, but that wouldn't have to last forever. One day he'd be known for exactly who and what he was. Then people would be dying to experience his story in VR! It would be a smart move to have it ready to download when the time came.

He reached the offices he'd found, and keyed in his entry. Normally this was done using the Ident-Chip embedded in people's wrists when they were hours old. But he didn't have an IC, so he used old-fashioned code. Sometimes the good old ways were best. The door opened, and he stepped into his new domain.

It had been the *LunarNews* headquarters at one time, until it had gone out of business and closed down. Devon had discovered all of the facilities were still intact, and had rented the place. The owners probably thought he aimed to start up a new NetChannel from here, but that wasn't his intention. Still, the vast computing power and the Net access via the Newsbots were perfect for his plans. He stood in the control room, pleased with his buy. There was a wall of Screens, which was what he liked. Powering up the systems (money was no problem, since he could hack into anything he wanted, to pay for whatever he needed), he turned the Screens on to different subjects. He liked to have thirty or forty running at once, and had no problem at all listening to and watching one and ignoring the rest.

He needed to know what was happening. Had Earth-Net finally given in to his Doomsday Virus? If so, Earth itself would be in a wonderful state of chaos. Of course, it would be hard getting pictures of all the disasters, since all of Earth's systems would be down at once. He'd have to rely on hacking into some of the older spy satellites. Nobody used them anymore, not since the Unified Earth had been formed, but there were still a dozen or so that hadn't been cleaned up out of orbit yet, and he knew how to access them all.

As the Screens all came to life, however, each feeding from a different LunarNet news channel, he saw nothing at all mentioned about computer problems on Earth. And there were some feeds coming in from Earth itself, showing rescue efforts in New York City. If the Doomsday Virus *had* destroyed EarthNet, there wouldn't be any news, or any rescue efforts, either.

Something had gone wrong.

Devon felt a burst of anger and frustration. How could his Doomsday Virus have failed? He wanted to break something, hurt someone, cause a disaster somewhere so he'd feel better, but this wasn't the time for self-indulgence. He could do that later. Right now, he needed information more than anything else. Besides, he had a good suspicion what had happened.

Tristan Connor. Somehow that dumb clone of his had gotten lucky.

It took him all of ten minutes to verify his suspicions. He checked out his old computers at Overlook and found that they were irretrievably dead. That was good news, actually, because it meant that nobody could find anything in his systems that he might have overlooked. He had everything he needed on carrier chips, and all he'd really left running back there was his Doomsday Virus generator. The only person who could possibly have stopped that was himself. Or, naturally, his identical clone.

He found Tristan's entry on the securitybots monitoring new arrivals. The boy had somehow survived Devon's careful murder plan and made his way to Overlook. It didn't take a genius to realize that he was the one responsible for shutting down the virus . . . and spoiling all of Devon's fun. The brat was becoming more and more annoying every minute.

It was time to deal with him personally, instead of getting underlings involved. Those thugs he'd sent to kill Tristan had somehow failed — twice! — to do the job. He was through relying on agents; this time, he'd deal with the fool himself.

The problem was that Tristan's IC wasn't registering anywhere on Overlook, and that didn't make much sense. At least, it didn't until Devon realized that it hadn't registered when Tristan arrived on the station, either. That meant the kid had somehow disabled it, and had to be using a fake chip for his transactions. Since it wasn't registering, it could only have come from one of the thugs Devon had sent to dispose of Tristan. Wonderful — not! The morons had not only failed, they'd managed to get themselves killed. Well, at least it meant they wouldn't talk.

Except, of course, in forensics . . . Devon had to get to their bodies before they could be examined. It wasn't at all possible that they could be traced back to him, of course — but they might be traced back to Quietus. Devon didn't want Quietus destroyed, since he had plans to take it over for himself.

First things first, though — where was Tristan? If he had a Quietus chip, the normal computer scans wouldn't be able to find him. But there hadn't been any departures from Overlook since Tristan had arrived, so he had to still be on the space station somewhere. It was just a matter of tracking him down.

Devon logged in to the station's monitoring system, and had the images flashed onto one of his Screens. He watched this with half his attention. Then he hacked into the schedule for departures. Nothing for two more hours. He had a special Screenwatch placed on the terminal for that. If Tristan showed up looking for a seat, Devon would find him.

Once that problem was dealt with, Devon turned to his next one. In order to take over Quietus, he would have to know a lot more about the group. Right now all he knew was that the Malefactor was one of the higher-ups in the organization. The Malefactor had been his sole contact with the group, and that link was now lost. Devon didn't know the real identity of the man — if it *was* a man and not a woman — or his location. But he had bugged the link the Malefactor had used, and he was certain that it had been untraceable. Devon was the only real computer genius in Quietus. Without him, they were just average people with dreams of grandeur. Actually, Devon didn't even know what their plans had been, mostly because he'd never been interested in them. Creating the virus and causing trouble were his main joys, and he now realized how foolish he'd been to limit himself to small pleasures like that when he should have been ruling the world.

In fact, he would be. Very, very soon.

He tapped into his own bug, and set it moving. It was slow because it couldn't afford to be spotted. But when it reached an access node, it would log on and connect up with Devon's lines here. Then he'd have the access he needed to get into Quietus without being spotted. And once he was there, he could begin finding out everything he needed. Names, places — and, most important — plans.

Then he could take them all over for himself. Instead of working for Quietus, Quietus would work for him.

Or it would die.

He scowled when he should have been happy. Where was Tristan? His double wasn't anywhere near as bright as Devon, so how could he still be hiding? The scanners had run through one time, and were starting again. There had been no sign of him. Nor was he in the flight terminal. There was no way he could have left Overlook by now.

Unless . . .

Maybe he'd found another way off the station. Not a

commercial flight, but something else? Devon hurriedly logged on to the main computer, and looked at everything that had been docked on the station for the past few hours. A repair flight, a satellite planter, anything . . .

He felt a terrible chill as the answer stared him in the face. A shield Ramjet had been docked for all of thirty-eight minutes. It had left the station only fifteen minutes ago. . . .

That *had* to be the explanation. Somehow the dumb shields had found Tristan! But were they helping him or arresting him? Devon's fingers flew over the speedboard as he tapped into the control systems, searching for answers. He wished he had his old, sophisticated, personalized Terminal now. That could get him anywhere much faster than this antiquated setup. Eventually, though, he managed to hack into shield headquarters. He scanned the warrants, and didn't see one for Tristan. Blast!

That meant that the shields must be helping him. And that could mean serious problems, because Tristan was the only person outside of Quietus who knew that Devon existed. If the shields found out . . .

He *had* to get everything erased, and fast. The only way to do that was to get at somebody inside Computer Control. He knew that Quietus had agents — and probably members — inside Control. One of those could deal with this situation, but Devon needed a name, and he needed it fast.

Otherwise, everything could still come crashing down around him.

He stared at his own reflection in the glass of one of the Screens. He had once thought that he was unique — the only person in the worlds who had that mass of hair, that slim, regal face, those penetrating eyes. But he had been wrong. Tristan looked exactly like him because he contained exactly the same genes. He had, after all, been cloned from Devon before Devon's birth. It was ironic that his own greatest problem was, in a strange way, himself. . . .

But he'd deal with Tristan soon. And then he'd have no further obstacles in his way.

4

Jame Wilson watched his father, Charle, at work with a sigh. His father was always busy these days, it seemed, but being deputy administrator here was, of course, a very important and responsible post. His father's dark hair was turning gray at the temples, and Jame sympathized. His father didn't look much like Jame, who rather liked his own dark hair and slender face. Sometimes, though, he wondered where he had inherited his looks. His mother didn't look like him, either.

Well, it wasn't important, but obviously what his father was doing was. Jame could see from here the strain on his father's face. Whatever was bothering him, he wouldn't talk about it. Nor would Mom, who was his father's secretary. "That's why we're called *secretaries*," she had told Jame. "Because we keep *secrets*!" A bad pun, but she meant it.

Jame decided that he'd go out instead. Syrtis was a wonderful place to live, and he never tired of exploring it. He liked using VR to "visit" other worlds; Earth, especially, could be very interesting to explore, since there was so much life and variety there. Mars was very different — the only life here was whatever had been brought up from Earth itself — and there wasn't a huge amount of variety, he supposed. You couldn't go outside the cities without environmental suits, since the air was still too thin to breathe.

One day, it would be different. When Mars had first been settled, some specially engineered viruses were brought up and released. They fed on some of the chemicals in Mars's crust, releasing oxygen into the air. After that, some very hardy plants had been seeded that could use the small amounts of oxygen to grow. There were small meadows of these plants now on the surface. One day, the whole planet would be filled with plants, and the air would be thick enough to breathe without using oxygen tanks. It probably wouldn't be for another hundred years, maybe even longer — the scientists themselves were only guessing, and the estimates kept changing. But one day, it would be possible to live on Mars in the same way people did on Earth.

Until then, residents of Mars were pretty much confined to the cities. Not that there were many — only seven so far, with Syrtis being the first, the biggest, and the official capital. Jame was one of the first people to live here, with his parents being almost in charge. It was style. Because of that, most people knew who he was, and he kind of liked that. He didn't have shields stopping him from poking around like many other kids did. He could go pretty much wherever he liked. Being a loner, he preferred to just take off on his own and examine things.

He'd discovered a lot about how the Administration managed to run things that way. He checked everything he could, and enjoyed it. He knew how restaurants worked, for example, and how the air was generated. He knew about the power grid, the radiation shields, and the spaceport. He had followed items from the time they were ordered over the Net until they were delivered, so he knew about the corridors that only 'bots ever used.

It was all fascinating to him. Jame loved knowing how things worked. One day, he knew, he wanted to be just like his father, helping to keep Mars running. So he'd made it his business to find out everything that might one day be useful. You could never know too much.

Today he decided he'd check out the docks. The word *docks* had once referred to wooden structures sticking out into the water on Earth, he'd discovered when he'd checked. There wasn't any water here on Mars, except in storage tanks deep underground, or frozen at the poles, so there weren't, technically, any real docks. But the word was still used to name the place where goods and people were unloaded from the spaceport. After all, *port* really meant a town on the waterfront, so "spaceport" was just as much a wrong name as docks!

It was always busy there, but today it was strangely more crowded than normal. What made this even odder was that there weren't any ships in the bay. He couldn't figure out why the workers were all gathered there, in that case. Surely they had packages and things in transit to take care of?

And then he realized that it wasn't just workers gathered here. There were also more shields than he'd ever seen before in his life, even the time he'd been shown around the shield building. And everyone seemed to be pretty steamed up about something. He moved in closer to get a better idea of what was going on. The shields had surrounded the workers, and nobody seemed very happy. The chief shield had just arrived, and was talking to one of the dock workers, a man Jame remembered was named Kristof.

"All of you," the shield said firmly, "go home. This is an unauthorized gathering."

"We just want some answers," Kristof said angrily. "Some word from the Administrator to reassure us that our jobs aren't in trouble."

"Your jobs will be fine," the shield said. "This is just a temporary shutdown. There are . . . problems with the shipments, that's all."

"There *aren't* any shipments!" one of the other workers yelled. "That's the problem! When will they start up again?"

"It's probably just a glitch in the system," the shield explained. "Due to this New York Net crash, I imagine."

"You have a good imagination," Kristof growled. "But we need *facts,* not imaginings. There are even stories that the whole of EarthNet is crashing, and that we'll be isolated up here on Mars." He gestured behind him at the workers. "My men and women have families to support; we need to know when we'll be paid again. We need answers from the Administrator, and he won't give them to us."

"Those stories are just rumors," the shield insisted.

"EarthNet is fine, and we're not cut off from them. I'm sure the shipments will start again soon, but until they do you must return to your domiciles."

"Not without guarantees!" a woman yelled. "I've two kids to feed, and they can't be fed on empty promises! We need pay, and work!"

"Listen to me!" the shield commander insisted. "You have to break up this meeting. I feel sorry for you, and I'm sure the Administrator is doing everything he can —"

"Then why isn't he here telling us that?" yelled one of the workers. "Why won't he give us *his* word?"

"He's doing everything he can," the shield answered again. "You're not the only ones with problems right now, you know."

"So," said Kristof with grim satisfaction, "there are *more* troubles that you people haven't told us about? What else should we know, then?"

"Go home," the shield pleaded. Jame realized the man was getting very strained and twitchy. He'd obviously been given his orders, and was trying hard to carry them out. But he was clearly out of his depth here.

"They're trying to stop us from even talking," the woman yelled to the rest of the workers. "They've got to be afraid that we'll find out the truth! They're lying to us — the shipments have stopped, and Mars is cut off!"

"That's not true!" the shield insisted. Then he made a bad mistake; he drew his tazer. "But you people *must* go home. Now!"

"Watch out!" one of the workers screamed. "They're going to kill us!" There was a moment of wild panic, and Jame crept back into the shadows, unable to stop watching. The workers started moving, some back toward safety, others forward toward the shields. Many were yelling out, either in panic or anger.

One of the workers drew a tazer of his own. "For Quietus!" he yelled, and then opened fire.

The shield commander gave a strangled cry and collapsed, his body smoking where it had been hit. There was a sudden, appalled silence as his corpse hit the floor. Then the rest of the shields pulled out their own tazers and returned fire. There was a stink in the air of ozone and badly burned flesh.

The worker with the tazer was the first to go down, but he wasn't the last. The shields seemed to have reached their limit, and were simply firing into the crowd. Jame saw Kristof fall, a shocked expression on his face. The woman with the two kids to support was cut down beside him. All the workers who could turned and fled, knocking down their comrades in the rush for safety. The shields stayed where they were, and eventually stopped firing.

Jame hugged the wall at his back, stunned and terrified by what he had just witnessed. There were bodies everywhere, mostly workers, but a couple of shields were down, too. The stench of death filled the air. Wanting to throw up, Jame turned and ran back to his home, his mind reeling. He needed some reassurance about what he had just seen, and only his father could give it to him.

When he reached their domicile, he saw that his father was in a meeting with the Administrator's hologram, and he would have to wait for ten minutes. He collapsed into a chair, shaking and sickened. He'd just watched people being killed, for no good reason. They had only been worried and scared, and had wanted to talk. That wasn't a good reason to kill them!

Finally, his father came out of his computer room, a worried expression on his face. He almost walked past Jame, but stopped and stared down at his son. Then he knelt beside the chair. "Jame," he said gently. "What's wrong? Are you ill?"

"No," Jame stammered. "I was just down by the docks. . . ."

"Oh, God." His father's eyes narrowed. "Did you see the riot?"

"I saw the killing," Jame confessed. He grabbed his father for comfort, and was hugged in return. "The shields just shot down the workers."

"The shields were attacked," his father said firmly. "They had no choice."

"No," Jame said. "I saw it. It was just one of the workers who shot at them, after the shield commander drew his gun. But the shields shot *everybody* they could, even unarmed ones!"

Jame's father held him at arm's length and stared at him. "You're wrong," he said gently. "The shields were fired on first. They only shot the workers with tazers. You should see the pile of guns they took from the dead."

"No," Jame insisted, shaking his head. "That's not how it happened. Honest, Dad."

"It *is* how it happened," his father insisted. "You just didn't see it all properly. Anyway, there's nothing for you to be worried about. The Administrator and I are dealing with the problem. He's declared martial law, which means that the shields will be in control for now. It won't affect you, except you may be stopped and searched sometimes by the shields. They're only looking for troublemakers, so it's nothing you have to worry about."

Jame couldn't believe what he was hearing. The shields had killed unarmed people, and his father was insisting they were some sort of rebels. And now the killer shields were going to be stopping people? He realized that they would also be arresting whomever they liked. They must have planted guns on the dead workers, to make it look like they had had a reason to kill them. What was going to stop them from doing the same thing to anyone else they didn't like? It was only their word that the people they would arrest were troublemakers — but nobody seemed to want to question their word.

Word . . . That reminded him. . . .

"There was one worker who shot at the shields," Jame recalled. "He yelled out something about . . . Quietus. Do you know what that is?"

"Quietus?" His father smiled slightly. "Of course I do, Jame. I'm a member of it. It's a group of people dedicated to setting everything that's gone wrong over the years right again. That worker must have heard about us, and wanted to stop us."

"No, Dad," Jame said. "He seemed to think he was *helping* Quietus by what he did."

"That's silly, son," his father said firmly. "Quietus isn't like that. I should know, because I've worked for them all of your life. So have you, in a way."

"Tell me more about it, then," Jame pleaded.

His father stood up. "Later," he promised. "Right

now, I'm afraid I have work to do. We have to hunt out the rest of these rebels and stop them before they start more riots. Don't worry, they won't get away with it. Everything will be fine." He paused by the door. "But, just to be on the safe side, don't leave our domicile until either I or your mom tells you, okay? See you soon." He left.

Jame collapsed back into the comfort of his chair. What his father had told him about the shields wasn't true; he'd *seen* what had happened. The shields had lied about what they'd done, and now they had been put in charge. That was crazy! They had to be stopped somehow, but Jame knew that there was nothing that he could do. He was just a fourteen-year-old kid who was really good with computers. He couldn't stop the shields on his own. And he didn't know who else would help him.

His father clearly wouldn't. For the first time in his life, Jame realized that his dad had let him down. It had never happened before, and it hurt him badly. His father hadn't believed his story; he'd accepted what the shields had said was true. Jame couldn't really blame him, but he knew his dad had made a bad mistake, and was making it worse by not listening to him.

What was going to happen to Mars now?

5

Inspector Shimoda was getting more and more nervous, even if she couldn't say why. She glanced at the pilot, who was impassively steering the Ramjet back down toward Newark's Schwarzenegger Space Port. Nothing seemed to be bothering him. Jill Barnes, on his other side, was looking as nervous as Shimoda felt. She also clearly thought that something was going to happen.

Shimoda twisted in her seat and checked the instruments again. They were only about fifteen minutes from landing now. Once they were on the ground, her troubles would probably just be starting. She and Barnes would be taking Tristan Connor to shield headquarters, and that was where the Quietus rats would probably try to strike. . . .

"Blast," the pilot suddenly complained, the first thing he'd said since they left Overlook. "The proximity radar is reading another aircraft. It's probably because the nav systems out of New York are down." He toggled his microphone. "This is Shield Flight 870. Please change your heading; you are about to enter our airspace."

Shimoda looked at the radar and saw the blip. According to the instruments, it was a small aircraft, rising from below them, heading on an intercept course.

This was no accident or malfunction, she realized. Quietus wasn't even going to wait until they were on the ground to strike.

"Evasive action!" she ordered. "They're after us."

"You've got to be joking," the pilot said, astonished. "Who'd be crazy enough to attack a shield jet?"

"They would," Barnes snapped, her eyes locked on the radar. "They're not changing course."

"Guns," Shimoda said firmly. Barnes nodded, and the two of them immediately locked in their weapons controls. Shield Ramjets weren't heavily armored or armed, because nobody in his right mind would think of attacking one. Until now. But there were two small gun turrets on the craft, so she and Barnes took command of one. The turrets were normally retracted to make the ship aerodynamic; now they were extended and ready. Shimoda slipped on the sighting helmet, and was looking out of the shield ship through the computer's eyes and other senses.

For a moment, it was as if Shimoda was disembodied and whipping through the air. She could feel the joystick that controlled the guns, but saw nothing but clouds below her.

Then the plane appeared, zipping straight toward them from below. That was Barnes's side, so Shimoda tensed but did nothing. The other ship was also a shield Ramjet. Clearly, it was manned by shields working for Quietus. It meant that they would be as well-armed as Shimoda's ship was.

She saw the tiny missiles streaking toward them from the other ship. Immediately, the computer started to lock on to them. Shimoda triggered return fire, working to cut down the missiles before they could hit her ship. Whenever the computer targeted one, it appeared in a halo of figures, and she'd tap the trigger to launch her own missile.

As she did, she was vaguely aware that Barnes was firing her own missiles at the other Ramjet, trying to bring it down. And the pilot was twisting and spinning their ship, attempting to avoid any of the other missiles locking on.

There were bursts of explosions in the air as she intercepted the attacking missiles. She couldn't afford to let any get through. She knew one hit could rip off half a wing, or worse. Thankfully, she and the computer worked well together, and she managed to catch all of the attacks before they got too close. Meanwhile, a halo of explosions was surrounding the attacking ship, too, as they fought back against Barnes's attack.

And then the other Ramjet whipped past them. They were clearly trying to go into a turn so they could come back for another attempt. Shimoda suppressed any pity she felt for the people in the jet; they were her enemies, trying to kill her and her prisoner. The fact that they were shields who were working for the enemy only made it worse — for them.

She targeted the underside of the other Ramjet and opened fire as it passed by.

Its pilot tried to dodge, and the gunmen aboard it tried to get all of her missiles. But she was better at this than they were. Four of her shots made it past their defenses.

The Ramjet seemed to simply disintegrate, falling into several sections before it was suddenly engulfed in flames. As she stared at it, trying not to feel sorry for the people onboard, the blazing wreckage began to fall from the sky, raining fire toward the ground, far below. Savagely, she ripped off her helmet.

"Nice shooting," the pilot said appreciatively, returning to their original flight path. "We'll be down in ten minutes. Think there'll be another attack?"

"This close to the ground?" Shimoda shook her head. "No. You'll be fine. I'm just worried about when I get my prisoner on the ground."

"I can call in shield protection," the pilot offered.

"*They* were shields," Barnes snarled, gesturing into the air. "I don't think we can be sure any shields coming to us would be on our side."

The man looked confused and then unsettled. "Our own men are trying to stop you?" he asked incredulously.

"Only a few of them," Shimoda informed him. "The problem is, we don't know *which* few. We can't rely on many people right now."

"You can rely on me," the pilot vowed. "I'll help you with the prisoner transfer."

"Thanks." Shimoda was sure he could be trusted, because if he was an agent of Quietus he could have managed to dispose of all of them by now. He was the only one still wearing a space suit; all he had to do was to open an airlock while they were in space, and she, Barnes, and Tristan would all die immediately.

They landed at the shield building without further trouble, where Shimoda's flitter was still waiting. Barnes jumped to her feet as soon as the Ramjet came to a halt. "I'll check out the car," she offered. "It may have been rigged to kill us while we were gone."

"Good thinking," Shimoda said approvingly. "I'll get Connor." She went back to the cell, and unlocked it. The boy was still in fetters, which would be enough to hold him.

"What happened out there?" he asked, looking shaken.

"Some friends of yours just tried to kill us," she replied.

"Then doesn't that prove they're not *my* friends?" he asked.

"No; it just proves they don't want you to tell us anything you know." Shimoda smiled grimly. "Don't you feel bad? They consider you expendable. Why don't you confess? Why protect those people? Tell me who else is working for Quietus. A kind word from me might influence your sentence."

"I can't tell you anything because I don't *know* anything," Tristan insisted. "I'm not a member of Quietus, and I don't know who is. Except for my clone, and some guy named the Malefactor. They're the ones you should be going after, not me."

Shimoda sighed. She hadn't really expected Tristan to tell her the truth or to cooperate, but it had been worth a try. "They're going to try to kill you again," she informed him. "I can help you stay alive if you help me stop them."

"Believe me," he snapped, "if I could, I would. But I don't know anything."

"Have it your own way." She led him outside, to where Barnes and the pilot were waiting with a different flitter.

"There's a small bomb in your old one," Barnes said pointedly. "I thought a new one would be safer."

The pilot nodded. "I've checked this out, and it's clean. You weren't kidding when you said there are traitors in our ranks."

"Keep alert," Shimoda ordered them both. "This isn't likely to get any safer. These people are fanatics, and they'll probably keep on trying to get him — and us in the process."

But, surprisingly, there were no further attacks. Perhaps Quietus was trying to lull them into a false sense of security; or perhaps they didn't really have that many agents in the shields, after all. Whatever the reason, they made it back to headquarters safely. Once there,

Shimoda had Connor transferred into the judicial system. Judge Montoya, who had been the one who had sentenced Tristan's girlfriend, Mora, was assigned. Shimoda turned to Barnes and the pilot.

"If you're up to it," she said, "could you take Connor down for trial? I have to have a few words with Chen right now, before the man can do anything else."

"We'll look after him," Barnes promised. She grinned. "Punch Chen in the eye for me, will you?"

"Chen?" the pilot asked, confused again. "What's the problem with him?"

"He was the only person who knew we were bringing in Connor," Shimoda explained. "He has to be the main traitor."

"Grief," the pilot muttered, clearly shaken. "Then punch him for me, too."

Shimoda nodded tightly, and hurried down the corridors. She wasn't going to see Chen directly, however. She ignored what was going on all around her; Quietus was hardly going to try to have her killed here in shield headquarters; there were simply too many honest shields around. She'd be safe for the time being, but she had to prevent further problems.

She strode into the outer office of Martin Van Dreelen, vice president of Computer Control, the board that effectively ran everything on Earth. Though Peter Chen was the head of security, Van Dreelen was his boss on the board. The secretary in the office looked up, a pinched expression on his face. "I'm afraid you can't —"

"Don't tell me what I can and cannot do," Shimoda said in a soft, dangerous voice. "This is a priority emergency, and if you try to get in my way, I'll be forced to tazer you. It'll no doubt ruin that pretty shirt you're wearing, and it might also land you in the hospital."

The secretary looked shocked, but didn't say another word as Shimoda crossed the office and opened the inner door. Van Dreelen himself was physically present, working on his desk-comp. He looked startled, especially when he saw the expression on her face.

"Inspector Shimoda, isn't it?" he asked, closing down his Screen. "I don't think we have an appointment. . . ."

"I'm sorry for the intrusion, sir," she said crisply. "But I'm afraid I have no option. I want you to have a warrant issued for the arrest of Peter Chen."

Van Dreelen looked startled again, which was hardly surprising. But he was a smart man, and realized quickly that there was a serious problem. "I assume you have good reasons for making such an . . . unprecedented request?"

"Yes, sir, I do." She gestured at his Terminal. "If I can just gain access to my files?"

"Of course." He moved aside but watched her like a hawk. That wasn't surprising, as he had no real reason to trust her yet.

"I suspected that there was a traitor in our organization," she explained, opening up her secret files and bringing them onto his monitor. She began to show him her evidence. "Somebody has illegally cloned Mr. Borden," she said. "The clone's body is down in the morgue right now. When I identified the person who created and used the Doomsday Virus as Tristan Connor, the boy was protected. . . ." She told him everything that followed, including the attack on her Ramjet. "The only person who even knew I had Connor on the ship was Chen," she finished. "Add this attack to his apparent lapse in normal procedure that allowed Connor to elude us for so long, as well as the clone of Borden, and you'll see that only Chen could have been behind it all. He's the reason we've been having so much trouble identifying Quietus and solving our problems. He was able to block us at every turn, until he finally made enough errors that I could prove."

Van Dreelen nodded. "Excuse me," he said, taking back the Terminal. "I'm issuing the warrant right now," he explained. "Take two more shields and arrest him immediately. I'll join you in his office as soon as the warrant is finished." He smiled warmly at her. "Well done, Inspector. Despite every problem placed before you, you have not only captured that murdering hacker, but exposed a renegade in our own ranks. This will not go unrewarded, I promise you."

"Thank you, sir." She hurried from his office, past the still-scared secretary, and back to her own section of the building. On the way, she grabbed two officers as they passed her in the corridor. Ignoring their protests of having other work, she made them go with her.

Chen's office was very similar to Van Dreelen's, only a little less luxurious. Tamra, his secretary, knew Shimoda well, of course. "Taki? I'm afraid that Mr. Chen is —"

"In serious trouble," Shimoda finished. She removed her tazer. "Don't interfere." She opened the inner door.

Chen was in teleconference with several other officers, and looked up, shocked, as Shimoda burst in. "Turn it off," she ordered.

"What is the meaning of this?" Chen demanded, starting to rise. He stopped when Shimoda pointed the weapon at him.

"You're under arrest, Chen," Shimoda informed him coldly. "For murder, attempted murder, corruption, selling state secrets, and God knows how many other charges." The two holo-officers looked startled, and both promptly cut transmission from their end. Their images vanished; they obviously didn't want to be included in the arrests.

"You're out of your mind," Chen snapped. This time, ignoring the tazer, he got to his feet. "You don't have the authority for this."

"She doesn't," Van Dreelen agreed, stepping into the room. "But I do, Chen. She's presented me with her evidence of your corruption, and I find it overwhelming, to say the least. There's absolutely no doubt in my mind that you're guilty." He held out a hand-comp. "Here's the warrant for your arrest." He turned to the two shields with Shimoda. "Take this piece of garbage to a cell and process the warrant. I want him Iced just as soon as it can be arranged." The two men saluted, and took the warrant.

Chen seemed to collapse inwardly. His shoulders sagged and he sighed heavily. "You're making a big mistake," he insisted, but there wasn't much fire in his voice.

"Can you explain any of my charges?" Shimoda challenged him.

"No," he admitted in a soft, defeated voice.

"Take him away," Van Dreelen repeated, a growl in his voice. Chen was led out of the office, and then the vice president turned to face Shimoda. "Now that the trash has been taken out," he said with a slight smile, "it does leave us with a slight vacuum." He gestured at the office. "Mr. Chen must be replaced, and I can't think of anyone better suited to it than the person responsible for exposing him and capturing our cyber killer — you, Inspector."

"Me?" Shimoda realized her voice was squeaking. She was too shocked to even think for a moment. Then she managed to settle down slightly. "But . . . there are a lot of people who are *much* more qualified than I am," she protested. "I'm just a shield."

"Miss Shimoda, don't be so modest. We all have to start somewhere." Van Dreelen smiled. "The problem is that most of the people under Chen who would normally be next in line for this office are his appointees. I am sure that most of them are in no way associated with his treason, but we cannot know which, if any, are not clean. You, on the other hand, most assuredly are. And you not only exposed Chen, but you also captured Connor, the boy who killed New York." He rubbed his hands together. "Now, being a politician, I recognize an opportunity when I see one. You'll be a media gold mine, young lady, the heroine of the day. Appointing you to Chen's office will be seen as a perfect example of inspired promoting. It will not only do you good, it will make me look good. So I simply won't allow you to say no." He gestured around the office again. "Get used to this place, Miss Shimoda — it's yours now." He turned to leave. "I'll let you get used to it. I'm sure his secretary can bring you up to speed here. If you have any problems, contact me directly. I know it'll take a couple of days for you to get used to things, but do your best. Oh, and one last thing — you'd better have someone take over whatever cases you were working on. You won't have the time for normal police work now." He grinned again. "Congratulations on your new position, Miss Shimoda. When you're settled in, we must go out for dinner. I have to get to know such a remarkably capable young lady better." He nodded at her and left.

Shaken, startled, and stunned, Shimoda collapsed into Chen's still-warm chair, and stared blankly out at the room. *Her* room. She was now head of security. . . .

It was too much to take in. And it was something she had never, ever considered. She wasn't stupid, and she knew that Van Dreelen's reasons for promoting her were exactly the opposite of what he had claimed. He wanted the publicity mostly. Having his old head of security exposed as a traitor and would-be killer would have been horribly bad news; Van Dreelen had managed to mitigate it a bit by promoting the brave shield who had uncovered Chen's treason. That would be wonderfully good news.

Politicians!

But what was she going to do next?

Tamra tapped on the door gently, and walked timidly into the room. "Congratulations on your promotion, Miss Shimoda," she said. She was trying to smile, but still looked shocked. It couldn't have been easy, seeing her boss carried off under arrest.

"Believe me, Tamra," Shimoda replied, "I didn't want it or expect it. I'm a victim of the political system. But since I'm stuck with it, and you're stuck with me, you're going to have to help me. I don't have a clue what I'm supposed to do, and I'm absolutely certain you know everything that Chen did. So — help!"

Tamra chuckled at this. "Okay, Taki — uh, *Miss* Shimoda."

"Just call me Taki, as always," Shimoda insisted. "Otherwise I'll be looking around to see who you're talking to. I'm really out of my depth here, Tamra, and I need you to help me out. Please!"

6

Mora had never in her life felt anything like this. She huddled, shivering, under the thin blanket that was her only protection from the cold night air. She and her parents had found an abandoned building here in the Underworld that offered them a little shelter, but nothing else. Her parents had lapsed almost into unconsciousness, simply sitting there, staring into space. Mora knew why — since they had been condemned to the Underworld by the justice system, they had lost everything. Only a few days ago, they had been moderately wealthy, with a lovely house, nice friends, and a future. They had celebrated her kid sister Marka's birthday with an elaborate party and lots of food. . . .

Food!

Mora's stomach was a tight knot of pain. She was so hungry her stomach had stopped growling. Her mouth was dry because all she'd been able to drink was stagnant water from an old puddle. There were no faucets down here, no shops with food, and no electricity for warmth and light, unless you found a way to harness it yourself. Tired, miserable, hungry, thirsty, and cold, Mora struggled to keep her mind.

It was all Tristan Connor's fault! It was hard for her to remember that at one time he was her boyfriend, and everything had seemed to be so right. They were very happy together, and she had planned on them going to college and then getting married and starting a family. . . . Now all she wanted to do was to make him suffer for what he had put her and her parents through. The only small blessing in this was Marka wasn't here. She'd been sent to live with an aunt.

Worried, Mora glanced at her parents. They were in terrible shape, hollow-eyed and pale. She doubted she looked any better. Her! She'd been widely acknowledged as the prettiest girl in her school, but if anyone saw her now, they'd scream in horror. Her hair was thick and stringy, her face smudged and pale.

She and her parents couldn't survive alone down here, that was clear. They couldn't find food or water. And they had no protection from the vermin that lived here — both animal and human. There was no law in the Underworld; if anyone wanted to kill her, they could do it without any fear of punishment. What she needed was someone who knew how to make things happen. And there was only one person she could go to.

Barker. The thief who'd robbed them when they arrived, and then had the nerve to offer her a job. Back then, she had righteously refused him. Now . . . well, what other choice did she have? She clambered to her feet, weak from hunger. "I'll be back soon," she promised her parents, hoping that she was telling them the truth. They didn't answer, and she wasn't sure they had even heard her.

The street outside froze her bare feet. Her skin was cut and bruised already, so she barely felt any further injuries. Limping, trying to ignore the pain in her stomach, she headed back toward the place where they had first run into Barker. He controlled this whole area, he had said, and his men would bring her to him if she asked. She could only pray that it would be his men she'd find, and not some other scavengers.

It was horribly oppressive down here, forty to eighty feet beneath the streets of the real New York. The roads and buildings above blocked almost all of the light from coming down. And, with New York Net down, few of the buildings over them had any power, so their lights — which might have shed a little illumination — were out, too. Mora realized that the people still trapped in their apartments over her head were probably in no better shape than she was. Good. She thought they deserved to suffer. Especially since they, at least, might look forward to rescue; there was nobody coming to save her.

There was a twitch of movement ahead of her, and then two thugs stepped out of the deep blackness of a building. Both looked at her, but neither spoke.

Summoning all of her courage, Mora held her head up and stared back at them. "I want to see Barker," she said. Was she right? Were these his men? Or was she in worse trouble? There was a short pause, and then one of the men stepped aside, gesturing for her to follow him. He walked back into the building. Mora hesitated a moment. Maybe he was taking her to Barker, as she'd asked. Maybe he intended to kill her. Then she decided she didn't care. Being dead would be better than remaining like this. She'd had all of her resistence beaten out of her these past few days.

She followed the man inside.

There was light in here, well hidden so that it couldn't

be seen from the streets. The place looked as filthy as anywhere else down here, but the thug wove through the mess with an air of much practice. Trying not to step on nails or anything else sharp, Mora followed.

There was a door at the end of the passageway, and he tapped on it in a very practiced manner, obviously code. The door opened, and the man gestured for her to go in. He waited outside, clearly aiming to return to his companion on guard duty.

Inside the room, everything was different. The place was well-lit, with a surprising amount of electricity. The place was old-fashioned, from almost a hundred years ago, back in the 1990s. The wallpaper looked fine, even if it was flaking in a few places. There were chairs and tables here, and several men sitting at them. They looked at her without much interest; they probably saw people like her every day and ignored them. One man was standing, looking her over.

"You here to see Barker, then?" he asked.

"Yes." Mora tried to look dignified, but it wasn't easy in her tattered blanket. She refused to show either fear or deference to these men.

"Right, come on." He led the way down a short corridor and then into another room. This one was a study, with a large desk, filing cabinets, and cases filled with books. There had been windows here once, for when the room had looked out on old New York, but they had long since been boarded over to stop light from getting out. Tall lamps lit the room. There were real paintings on the walls.

Barker was behind the desk, and a youngish-looking woman was relaxing on a sofa nearby. Mora recognized the dress the woman was wearing; it had been her mother's until Barker had taken it as spoils of war. Barker himself was middle-aged and lean. A smile that looked to be genuine lit his face. "Ah, our latest sewer rat! Come to your senses, hey, girl?"

"I don't think being down here leaves you with any senses," Mora answered.

Barker wasn't offended by her remark, and laughed. "Still got some spirit, at any rate. Well, then, girl, why are you here?"

Mora's throat was too dry to even allow her to swallow. "You offered me a job," she reminded him.

"And you turned me down," he replied. "Rather forcefully, I might add."

"I've changed my mind."

"So I gather." He got up from his seat. "Hungry? Cold? Thirsty? Scared?"

"All of them."

Barker nodded. "I knew you would be." He looked at her critically. "Down here, the rules are very different from the world you knew, girl. Down here, you have to live my way. Otherwise you don't live at all. Are you ready to do whatever I ask of you now, in exchange for my protection?"

"No," Mora said honestly. "Look, I could lie to you and say yes, but there's no point, is there? There are some things I won't do, not even to stay alive. So if you're going to ask any of those of me — well, just have one of your men slit my throat, or something."

At this, the woman laughed. "She's got you there, Sammy, hasn't she?"

"So it would seem." Barker was obviously amused. "All right, girl," he said. "Lick my shoes clean."

Mora didn't even glance down at them. "No."

"And why not? Too high and mighty still?"

"Partly," she said. "And partly I'm so thirsty I don't have any spit left in me."

Rather proudly, Barker turned to the woman. "You see, Lili? She's almost as sharp-tongued as you, and she's bright. We could use her." He looked back at Mora. "All right, girl. I like you, even if you still think you're all that. We'll knock that out of you in time. You have to understand that I may be in charge of things here, but I'm mostly in charge of a bunch of thugs and yes-men who don't have two ideas to rub together between them. I need somebody else besides me and Lili here who can think." He sighed. "It's relatively easy and simple being a thug, you see, and my men are good at it. But planning — that's as far beyond them as the stars. You're a smart girl, and if you work with me and Lili, I think we could make my enterprises a lot more successful. What do you say, eh?"

"Three things," Mora answered. "First, my name's Mora, not *girl*. Second, you look after my parents as well as me. And third — well, I *really* want to change my look." She shuddered. "This blanket and the starving thing is *so* not me, you understand?"

"Perfectly," Barker agreed. "Lili, take young Mora here and get her fixed up. Food and drink first. Then, I think, a bath. No offense, Mora, but you stink."

"Don't I know it?" She felt as if her life was returning to her now. "That sounds wonderful."

"Then some better clothes, obviously, and a little help for your family," Lili said, putting a sympathetic arm around Mora's shoulders. "Anything else you want?"

"Yes," Mora said. "But it's something even Barker can't supply. I want to make a boy named Tristan Connor suffer."

"Well, we'll see what we can do about that," Lili said. "Let's get to the important things first."

"That is important to me," Mora told her. "But it can wait . . . for now."

7

Tristan's head was in a whirl. He'd been arrested and then marched through shield headquarters by two officers. They'd deposited him in another cell and waited outside, obviously prepared for trouble. However, nothing happened, and after a short wait they escorted him out of the cell and into the courtroom.

Judge Montoya was already waiting, along with two men. The shields pushed Tristan into a small stand, and waited impassively beside him.

"New York Supreme Court," one of the men announced. "Judge Montoya presiding." Tristan realized that this was being recorded, obviously for posterity and most likely for the NewsNets, too. The capture and trial of the "villain" responsible for destroying New York City was immensely important news. The fact that he was actually innocent was incidental. "The accused is Tristan Connor; the crime, that of Net sabotage."

Montoya was an elderly woman with a harsh-looking face. "This is the worst crime it has ever been my misfortune to be forced to try," she said solemnly. Obviously, she wanted to get her share of time on the Nets! "We still have no tally for the final loss of life that this disaster caused New York City, but it must number in the thousands. There are still people trapped in their homes and offices, and the power grid, water, and Net are still down. This has been a disaster of incredible proportions." She glared at Tristan. "How do you plead?"

"I'm innocent," he said firmly. "The shields got the wrong person."

"Really?" Judge Montoya looked at her Screen. "They have your fingerprints and DNA all over the computer that originated the Doomsday Virus. You were on-line each time it was released, and you were actually captured destroying all of the evidence on your Terminal. How, then, could they have taken the wrong person?"

"Because the *right* person is my double," Tristan informed her. "We're identical. His name is Devon, and he works for a subversive group named Quietus. He claims that I'm his clone, but I'm not sure if that's the truth. But we *are* identical, down to our DNA and finger-prints."

"I see," Montoya said. "In other words, it wasn't you who did it but an exact duplicate of you. One whom no-body has ever seen? And one who can't be traced at this moment?"

"Well, yes." Tristan did realize how lame this sounded. "Look, Inspector Shimoda said you'd be able to prove this really simply. You just give me this truth-telling drug, Truzac, and then question me. I'll have to tell the truth, and it'll be what I just told you."

"Your honor," the second man said, stepping for-ward, "we feel that this is a pointless idea. Truzac only works if the person being questioned *knows* the truth. It is my opinion that this young man may well believe that he has a mythical clone, and he's created this clone in his own mind, so to speak. It's classic mental sickness — Connor can't accept responsibility for his own actions, so he's created a mythical monster in his mind that looks like him, but is, he believes, evil. So if we gave him Truzac, he would indeed repeat this non-sensical story of his because he most likely firmly be-lieves in the truth of what he's saying. As you have already noted, there is nothing to even suggest that this person Devon actually exists. He cannot be found and has never been seen by anyone. Only Tristan Connor claims to have seen him, and his guilt is more than proven by the evidence."

The judge considered this, then nodded. "I'm inclined to agree with you here. To have committed such crimes as he has, Tristan Connor *must* be mentally ill. In which case the use of Truzac would be pointless." She stared at Tristan. "Guilty as charged."

"What?" Tristan could hardly believe what he was hearing. "Your Honor, that's not right! I *am* telling the truth! I *didn't* do what you've accused me of."

"Not *accused*," the judge said grimly. "*Convicted*." She shook her head. "The only possible sentence for what you have done is life on Ice without any parole. Considering what you've done and the many, many lives you've wrecked, I wish I could do more. You don't deserve to live, Connor. But that option isn't open to me, because of the Hynde case of 2036. You'll be forced to live with whatever shreds of conscience you have left for the remainder of your life, never to walk among decent people again." She rapped the bench with her formal gavel. "Take him away. He makes me sick."

Tristan tried again to protest, but there really wasn't any point. The two shields took one arm each and marched him out of the courtroom. He was too numb to resist. He had never thought that this could possibly happen. He had been certain that whoever was in charge would listen to his story, and that he'd be proven right and set free.

Now he was a convicted criminal, sentenced to spend the rest of his life rotting in jail. Somewhere, he knew, Devon had to be laughing about this. He was the only person who *would* be laughing, though. Because without Tristan free to stop him, the next time Devon struck, he'd manage to do more than destroy a single city. He might well destroy all of human civilization.

And there was nothing that Tristan could do about it.

Judge Montoya left the courtroom for her own private chambers. There, her Terminal chimed. "You have a call," it informed her.

"Accept," she said. She had a suspicion that this was the call she'd been expecting. The ominous black shape of the Malefactor sprang to life before her. "You took your time," she said coldly.

"I came as soon as I could, Controller." As always, his voice was muffled and computer-changed. As if she didn't know who he really was! The man's habitual secrecy was as stupid as the rest of his personality. But he was necessary to Quietus, so she tolerated it — barely. "What news do you have for me?"

"Only that I've tied all of your problems neatly to-gether for you to *finally* deal with," she informed him. "Tristan Connor was just in my court."

"And what did you do with him? Do you still have him?" The Malefactor sounded eager.

Montoya sighed; it was like dealing with a child. "Of course not, you idiot. The shields are already looking for Quietus agents inside their own ranks. I can't afford to draw any attention to myself. Connor was charged and processed, so I had to deal with him reasonably. I did manage to block the use of Truzac, of course. He knows a lot more than he was ever supposed to. And I still don't know how he managed to get here from Mars without anybody noticing."

"Nor do I," the Malefactor answered. "Yet. I spoke with his father, Charle Wilson, and the man had the nerve to claim that Jame is still on Mars! But what did you do with him, then?"

"I sentenced him to life in Ice," the judge answered. "He'll be there by the end of the day. Since I already sentenced that interfering girl Genia there, you'll have both of your problems under one roof, so to speak. All you have to do is to organize a . . . rescue party to get them out of there and dispose of them properly. That will tie up all of our loose ends." She thought a mo-ment. "Oh, yes — that Mora Worth girl and her family. I thought they might know something, that Connor may have spoken some of his suspicions to them. So I sentenced them to the Underworld. They're probably dead by now. I doubt they know anything useful, but I don't like to take chances." She smirked. "You're lucky I'm here to help you cover up your mistakes."

"You'd better be careful what you say," the Malefactor growled. "You've been useful to me in this matter, and I will see to it that the . . . *problems* are taken care of. But don't start thinking you can make me look bad to Quietus, Controller. Don't forget, I know where *your* bodies are buried, too."

"Don't try threatening me, Malefactor," Montoya told him. "You've been making so many mistakes in this matter that I don't *need* to bad-mouth you to Quietus. You're doing a wonderful job of it all by yourself. Oh, and speaking of *by yourself,* have you managed to rein in Devon yet?"

There was the slightest pause before the Malefactor replied, "He's been dealt with for now. I don't wish to punish him unduly, since we're likely to have to destroy his clone brother, and we'll need Devon all the more now."

"What about the other clones?" Montoya asked. "There were twelve of them originally produced. Can't we activate one of the ten remaining clones?"

The Malefactor sighed. "That would delay our plans another fourteen years," he pointed out. "And I, for one, am getting very impatient. It's much simpler to deal with Devon. If nothing else succeeds, then I'll have his mind wiped. That way, we can still use his DNA to access everything that we need."

"I hope you're right." Montoya glared at his image. "The Doomsday Virus has been defeated, as you must surely be aware by now. It has been wiped out of the Net. And Connor destroyed the generator."

The Malefactor smiled. "But I managed to trick him into sending a refined version of the virus to me," he gloated. "He thought it would self-destruct, but I have it preserved. When the time is right, the virus can be . . ." His voice trailed away. "*Connor* destroyed the virus?"

"Of course he did, you fool. Who did you think . . . ?" Awareness suddenly dawned on her. "You thought it was *Devon*? You idiot! That was Connor in Devon's apartment." Her voice hardened. "Where is Devon? If he wasn't there, you'd better not have lost him. He's absolutely crucial to the rest of our plans now."

"I'll handle this," the Malefactor insisted. "It's just a temporary glitch. Besides, when my men recover Connor, we'll have access to all the cloned DNA we'll ever need."

"That's not the point right now," Montoya snarled. "If

Devon is missing, who knows what he could be up to? I always felt he was too unstable to be fully trusted. He was only safe while he was kept in his rooms. But the officers who arrested Connor found no trace at all of Devon, so he must be on the loose. Find him *immediately.*"

The Malefactor severed the connection without replying. Montoya took a deep breath. *The fool!* He'd lost Quietus's most valuable asset!

It was definitely time to start working on getting him removed. She smiled to herself. He was doing a wonderful job of messing everything up. She wouldn't even need to frame him for failure. . . .

Humming cheerfully, she turned back to her docket to see what work she had coming up. One eyebrow rose as she saw the name of Peter Chen. Calling up his case, she scanned the information. So he had been accused of being an agent of Quietus, had he? Well, she could deal with *that!*

8

Shimoda was feeling very lost in this huge new office, and she still didn't have much clue as to what she was supposed to do. But she had a few ideas about what she *could* do. She pulled up her own file, now that she had the authority to check on any of them. The first thing that astonished her was that it already had been updated to show her new rank. The second thing that amazed her was her new salary — almost three times as much as she had been previously paid. But when she started to check Chen's notes on her, astonishment turned to anger.

It was clear from his file that he thought of her as an

idiot. He scored her only average on computer skills, for example. Shimoda knew she wasn't a genius at them, but she was certainly better than average! This did make sense of a few things that had been bothering her, though. If he thought she wasn't very skilled at tracing criminals who used computer skills, then it explained why she'd been assigned to track down the villain behind the Doomsday Virus. Chen had expected her to fail — no, more than that, he *wanted* her to fail. Working for Quietus, he didn't want Connor to be found, of course, and he had to have been certain that she'd never be able to find him.

And that was why he'd been so furious when he had found out about Genia. The girl was a genuine genius with computers, and if she was working with Shimoda, then there was real danger that Connor would be tracked down. So he'd been forced to arrest her and send her for trial, hoping that Shimoda would fail without the girl's help.

But she hadn't failed. Not only that, she'd managed to prove that he was a traitor, too. As she read on, she realized that her boss hadn't liked her at all. If there was any possible way to downgrade her, he did it. She was aggressive and determined to catch criminals; he called her "pushy" and "bossy." She was tenacious, and he called her "stubborn." She was thorough and he called her "slow." She could see why she hadn't had a promotion for the past few years. . . .

Until now. She had Chen's job, and he was in jail. What goes around, comes around. . . .

Now that she had power, maybe it was time to start using it.

She called up Genia's file next. There wasn't much in it, of course, since she'd been unmonitored all her short life. Chen had noted her criminal past, however, including some video shots of Genia robbing a bank that had been taken from a Monitor across the street. The only other entry in the file was her trial. Grimly, Shimoda watched the replay of it. Under Truzac, Genia had been forced to tell the truth about her robberies, and she had, understandably, been convicted of theft and sent to Ice.

Well, the judge really hadn't had much choice there. The only other penalty option was to send Genia to the Underworld. Doing that to Genia was the equivalent of setting her free, though. She had a large apartment, sophisticated computer equipment, and a pretty decent lifestyle there. Sending Genia to Ice was the only punishment that would work.

Only Shimoda wasn't certain that the girl deserved it. True, she was a thief, but she'd never known any different life. She'd grown up in the Underworld, and there she had to steal or die. Shimoda thought a better sentence would have been supervised parole. Genia just needed an honest role model and a chance to work legitimately, and Shimoda was sure she could become a productive member of society. The girl wasn't really bad, just underprivileged.

Maybe she could put in a recommendation to the judge that Genia's sentence be changed. She felt guilty that she had let the girl down, and wanted to correct it. There was only one problem, and she forced herself to consider it. *Who* would agree to supervise Genia? If she asked the judge, Shimoda knew that there was only one person the judge would consider — Shimoda herself.

Shimoda wasn't certain that she wanted the complication of a young girl in her life. Especially now that she had this new job, with extra power and extra responsibility. It was bound to mean extra work, and she wouldn't have much time to spare for the girl. Genia needed someone who would be around when problems cropped up, not somebody who was working late at the office.

Maybe she could get Jill Barnes to consider it instead? But was that fair to the other woman? And would Genia even trust her? Come to think of it, would she trust Shimoda again?

Anyway, would the judge even consider changing the sentence? Shimoda had never heard of it happening, but that didn't mean it wasn't possible — only that it hadn't been done. She decided to check the judge's records, and see what she was like. If she was always tough on people, then she wouldn't be inclined to give Genia a chance. If she was generally pretty gentle on them, it was possible she had a soft spot that could be appealed to.

Shimoda called up Judge Montoya's last twenty-five cases to check. Then she gasped.

Montoya had not only sentenced Genia; she'd also sentenced Tristan.

And *Mora* and her parents . . . Shimoda didn't even know that they had been arrested!

Quickly, Shimoda scanned the trial, and was appalled at what she saw. The judge had not merely been harsh, she'd been savage. Sentencing Mora and her parents to the Underworld because one of them had *possibly* helped Tristan escape justice? That was not only unfair, it was borderline criminal. . . . And she hadn't allowed the prisoners to use Truzac, which *was* illegal.

What was going on here? Shimoda hesitated very briefly, and then called up Tristan's trial record.

It was even worse. Once again, he hadn't been given Truzac. Nor had he been given a chance to answer the charges. Shimoda was certain he was guilty, but that didn't excuse the fact that he'd been treated badly.

Montoya was up to something, that much was clear. Did she have the power to refuse Truzac to the accused? Shimoda didn't know, but there was one person who would. She placed a call to Van Dreelen. She only had to wait a few minutes before he responded, and she could project her image into his office.

The office was even richer than the one she'd been given, which made sense, of course. She wondered for a second how much *he* was making for a salary; three times her new one? Well, that didn't matter. "Sir," she said, "I've been doing some research, and I'm rather . . . disturbed by what I've discovered. I've been looking into recent cases tried by Judge Montoya."

Van Dreelen scowled slightly. "That's not really your department, Miss Shimoda," he replied. "You're in charge of Security, not Judicial."

"I know, sir," she agreed. "But it's just that she has been trying most of my recent cases. And in at least two of them, she didn't conduct the cases legally, as far as I can tell."

Now she had his attention. "You think she fixed the trials?" he asked sharply. "That would be a very serious accusation. I need some proof before I could possibly consider following up on this."

"I'm not saying she fixed the trials," Shimoda assured him. "She tried Connor's case, and I'm sure she was right to convict. But she didn't give him Truzac, even though he requested it. At the very least, he could have told us much more about this Quietus organization. Why didn't she have him questioned?"

Van Dreelen looked almost relieved. "Oh, so *that's* your problem." He spread his hands. "I understand that there has been some problems with the Truzac treatments. I'm no specialist, but it seems that some criminals have found ways around the serum. And in Connor's case, you will no doubt have noticed that the court's opinion was that he was schizoid, and might well believe his own story about there being an exact double of him around."

"Taking the last first," Shimoda answered, "Connor didn't seem in any way mentally ill, sir. He simply lacks a normal conscience and probably thinks he's better than everyone else. But that's not schizoid behavior. He should have been given Truzac so we'd have his testimony, at least."

"What's the point in giving it to him if we can't believe what he says?"

"I'm having a hard time believing that anyone can beat Truzac," Shimoda confessed. "It was given to that girl, Genia, and she confessed promptly and accurately. Why should it work on her and not on Connor?"

"As I said, I'm not a specialist," Van Dreelen replied.

"But if it works only on certain people, I believe that there's a problem. I have a report on the problem somewhere. I'll have a copy sent to you. I don't think that there's been an error here, to be honest. But, then, I didn't think there was anything wrong with Chen, either, did I? I could be wrong again. Check the report out thoroughly and let me know what you think. I don't feel we have any real reason to believe that Judge Montoya is a problem — at least, not yet. She *is* following department guidelines. But if she's somehow twisting them for her own purposes, we need to know. So keep your investigation of her open." He sighed. "I'm starting to wonder just whom around here I can trust."

"Join the club," Shimoda commented.

He was too smart to pretend he missed the point of *that* remark. Raising an eyebrow, he studied her. "Am I to take it that you're wondering about *me* now?"

"Of course I am," she admitted honestly. "Giving a novice such a promotion as this . . ." She shrugged. "And especially considering what Chen put about me in my files. He's right about one thing, though — I'm not a computer genius. So why promote me?"

Van Dreelen laughed. "Well, that's one of the reasons, actually — because you're *not* a computer genius. Yes, I read your report. And I read between the lines. Chen didn't like you much, and it shows through.

I always disregard such opinions, and I've been watching you as you worked on this Connor case. You're no computer whiz, but you're smart, tenacious, and you know when to break the rules. You're more interested in getting to the truth than in simply doing your job. And, lastly, you're suspicious of everyone and everything. Since head of security has to be suspicious of everyone and everything, it seems to me you're ideal for the job." He grinned at her. "So, if you feel you have to suspect me, then go ahead and do your job. I know I'm innocent, so I'm not worried about what you'll find. Frankly, I think we'll make a very nice team."

Her cheeks blushed from the praise. "Thank you, sir. I'll pay attention to what you've suggested. And I'll try and get the rest of my job done properly, just as soon as I'm certain I know what it is."

"That's the spirit." He nodded, and closed down the link.

So — she'd told him her suspicions, and he had countered with reasonable replies. Was he telling the truth? Or was he playing her for a fool?

Only time would tell. . . .

9

Tristan stepped numbly into Ice, thankful at least to be out of the frigid Antarctic wind. He was starting to see why everyone considered the place to be escape-proof. Even if you could break out of the main jail, where could you go? It was set in the middle of the harshest climate in the world, and there was no way off the vast, frozen island. Nevertheless, he knew he was going to have to try and get out of here. He simply couldn't give in to despair and leave Devon to do whatever he wished. No matter what the world might think about Tristan Connor, Tristan couldn't turn his back on his duty.

Besides, he wanted to know the truth — about Quietus, about Devon, and about himself. Devon had claimed that Tristan was his clone. Was that true? Probably Devon believed it, but did he *know* it? Tristan had to uncover the secrets of his own past. Who — or what — was he really? Finding Devon might get him a step closer to himself.

On the flight from New York, Tristan had passed from despair to hope again. Not full hope yet, but the start of it. Maybe he wasn't the evil computer genius the shields thought — but he *was* a computer genius. If he could just get Net access again, then maybe he could find a way out of here. Of course, it was highly unlikely that the prisoners were allowed to have Terminals in their cells!

"Right," said the guard, breaking into Tristan's thoughts. "You're here, and here you'll stay. I think you've seen from the outside that there's no way out of here unless we let you go. And your sentence says that's *never* going to happen. So you'd better start getting used to this place. Once you're down in the cells, the inmates will let you know the rules, and you'd better follow them. The guards don't bother patrolling the cells much, so the other inmates tend to deal with people they don't like. Keep your nose clean and you should be fine. If you have any complaints — keep them to yourself. We're not interested, and we won't do anything about them. Any questions?"

"Would you answer them if I had any?" Tristan asked.

"Probably not." The guard grinned. "In you go." He gestured at the door behind him.

Tristan didn't have any choice, really. He walked through the door, and found himself in an elevator. It took him on a short journey and then opened into a large room. There were no guards in sight, but several prisoners. The room had been hollowed from the bare rock, and though there were heaters, it had a chill that reached into his bones.

"You Connor?" one of the men asked. Tristan nodded; he'd obviously been expected.

The punch caught him by surprise, knocking the breath out of him and sending him sprawling.

"You filthy menace!" the man growled. "I've got family in New York, and they might be dead because of you!" He grabbed a handful of Tristan's shirt, and backhanded him hard enough to draw blood.

"But I didn't . . ." Tristan protested. His mouth stung, and his ribs hurt.

A second man moved in and kicked him hard in the side. Tristan screamed from the pain. "Murderer!" the man yelled, and kicked him again.

Tristan lost count of the number of punches he took.

Two other men joined in beating him, and there was hardly a pause between blows or kicks. He tried to crawl away, but they followed, pummeling him without mercy. He was bleeding from several cuts, and his sides burned from the kicks. The pain was awful, but he couldn't defend himself and he couldn't fight back. It was simply a mass of agony, and all he could hope was that he'd pass out and not be able to feel anything else.

"Okay, lads, that's enough," a fresh voice said. Tristan could barely make out the words through the haze of pain. There were a couple of muttered curses, but the blows stopped.

"Come on, Marten," one of his attackers objected. "He's a filthy murderer."

"So are you, Samel," the newcomer said patiently. "We're all here because of crimes we committed."

"I only killed one man," Samel complained. "This rat killed thousands. Probably some of your kin, too. Don't you think he should suffer?"

"He *will* suffer," Marten agreed. "He's here for life, after all. And if you kill him now, then his suffering will be over. Leave him alone for now. You can always have another go later. But always let him live, otherwise how can you hurt him?"

"He's got a point," one of the other men agreed. "I

guess we've done enough for now." He spat on Tristan's face. "But keep looking over your shoulder, scum. One day, I'll be there, and I'll get some more in."

The other men muttered their agreement, and added further spittle to Tristan's wounds. Tristan could barely make them out through the red haze over his eyes. "Thank you," he gasped to his savior.

"Don't thank me," Marten said dryly. "I'm not sure I've done you a favor. They will be back, you know. Everyone here is guilty of some crime or other, but yours is one that none of them can stomach."

"I didn't do it," Tristan said slowly, hoping he didn't have any broken teeth or bones. It hurt to move, so he lay still.

"Right." Marten clearly didn't believe him. "Well, Genia, you wanted him; are you just going to stand there and look at him?"

"He's a bit of a mess," she said critically. Tristan twisted his head to look at where she was standing, behind Marten. She didn't look like anyone he'd ever seen before. Aside from the bright, almost glowing yellow jumpsuit she wore, she had thick, long, dark hair. He'd never seen any girl with hair longer than a few inches; hers was more than three times as long. Even though he was in pain, he thought it looked really good. If Mora grew her hair out . . .

Then she'd be losing it, and anyone could steal it and gain access to her computer accounts. Long hair might look nice, but it was horribly impractical. Still, he supposed that here such things didn't matter.

"Who are you?" he asked the girl.

"My name's Genia," she informed him. "You've caused me a lot of trouble with this virus of yours."

"It wasn't my virus," Tristan said wearily. "Though I don't expect you to believe that any more than anybody else has. Not even my girlfriend believes me, so why should you?"

"Do I detect some bitterness there?" Genia asked with a grin. "That's a language I speak fluently." She looked him over critically. "You're quite a mess." She turned to the man. "I guess we'd better help him to his cell and see if we can at least stop the bleeding. I'm sure they wouldn't bother with medical supplies down here, but —"

"Actually, you're wrong," Marten answered. "State-of-the-art equipment, in fact. They've got to be *humane* to us, after all. The only thing is, we don't have any doctors."

"Not a problem," Genia said with confidence. "I've been looking after myself for years. I'll see to his wounds. Come on."

It hurt when the two of them picked him up to move

him, but Tristan didn't cry out. At least they were trying to help him, even if he wasn't sure why. Neither of them seemed to particularly like him, and there was no reason why they should. He'd only just arrived, and they didn't know him at all.

They reached the infirmary after a couple of painful minutes. Tristan was glad to collapse onto a diagnostic bed. Genia looked puzzled when she saw its controls; obviously, whatever experience she had didn't include this. For once, Tristan was glad he'd been in the hospital recently. Wincing with pain, he reached over to turn on the diagnostic panel, and then lay back down while it hummed to itself.

"Right, well, I can do the next part," Genia informed him. "Strip to the waist, so I can put on No-Bleed and dressings." She had to help him do it, though, as his left arm was too sore to bend properly. "Wow, you're a mess," she said cheerfully. She began applying the lotion, and he had to force himself not to yelp each time she touched a tender spot. There were a lot of tender spots. Eventually, though, she was done. She examined the diagnostic panel. "You're quite lucky," she informed him.

"I don't feel lucky," he growled. "I hurt all over."

"Lots of bruising, but no broken bones. You'll just be sore for a while, though the bed says to give you a shot of medication to ease the pain and swelling." She looked around.

"Here," Marten said, opening a drawer. He took out a spraygun, and clipped in a measured dosage of the drug. Genia took it and sprayed it on Tristan's side. Marten grinned. "Maybe the two of you could make yourselves useful in here working in the infirmary?" he suggested. "You seem to know roughly what you're doing, which is more than any of the rest of us do." He stared pointedly at Tristan. "It might save you from future beatings."

"I'll keep that in mind," Tristan said. With Genia's help, he closed up his coveralls again. "But I don't want to stay here very long."

Marten laughed. "None of us do, but we don't have a lot of choice in the matter. You and my daughter seem to be of the same mind-frame here. You're both crazy. On which note, I'll leave you alone." He gave a mock salute and then left.

Genia was his daughter? Now that he knew, Tristan could see some resemblance between them; the same eyes, the same set to the jaw. "I don't have any option. I *have* to get out of here."

"And why's that?" asked Genia. "To prove your innocence?"

"That would be nice, but no." Sensing that she was

interested, he told her his complete story. "So I'm sure that Devon's got more nasty surprises planned for the world," he finished. "And since everybody thinks I'm guilty, nobody's even looking for him. So I've got to get out of here and capture him."

"Call me crazy, Tristan," she said, "but I believe you."

"You do?" Tristan was astonished. "That's a first. What makes you sure I'm telling the truth?"

"Because I experienced the virus and your stealth dogs firsthand. They're both coded in pretty much the same way, which they would be if you and Devon think along similar lines. But the stealth dogs lack the killer instinct of the virus. And — pardon me if this offends you — so do you. You're a wimp, going along with whatever happens to you. You don't have the guts to create a killer virus."

"Thanks, I think," said Tristan dryly.

"So this clone-twin of yours may be far-fetched, but it seems more likely to me than the idea that you're a callous mass murderer. Heck, if you ask me, you've got too many morals, not too few."

"Thanks, but I'll stick with what I have," Tristan said. "So what are you in for?"

"Trusting a cop," Genia informed him. "Oddly enough, Shimoda." She told him her story, bringing him up to date on her life. "So I want to get out of here, too," she finished. "Not for any crusade like yours. But to get back to my old life. So how about we team up? We're both computer whizzes — I'll bet that together nobody and nothing could stop us."

Tristan considered her offer. To have a friend here would be helpful, but he wasn't sure he wanted to help put any criminals back on the street. And by her own account, Genia was a very good crook. "I'll agree, on one condition."

"Only one?" Genia pouted. "I would have bet on at least ten."

Ignoring her insult, Tristan explained: "I have to find Devon and stop him. Nothing else much matters right now. I want you to promise to help me once we get out of here. Otherwise it's no deal."

"Has anyone ever told you you're obsessive?"

"Pretty much everyone I know. What do you say?"

"What's to stop me promising and then breaking my word? How do you know you can trust me?"

Tristan shrugged. "I don't, really. But I'm willing to bet that if you promise something, you'll stick to it. You don't seem like a liar to me."

"Just a thief and a swindler, eh?" Genia grinned and stuck out her hand. "I must be crazy, but okay — it's a deal. We work together from now on, until one or the other of us decides to go our separate ways. But it won't be until after we stop this Devon maniac. Fair enough?"

"Fair enough." He shook her hand. She might be a criminal, but he was actually starting to like her.

"And one last thing," she added. "Don't start looking at me to replace your lost girlfriend, okay? I don't do mushy stuff, and I *definitely* don't get attached to kids who are younger than me."

Tristan was offended. "Mora's not lost," he protested. "I'm sure she'll realize that what she did was wrong. I'll get her back again, I know it."

"Good," Genia said. "Focus on that thought. Now, are you up to moving? I happen to have access to a desk-comp, thanks to dear old Dad. We might as well get started. I have the feeling that this is the beginning of a very fruitful friendship."

10

Jame sat in the computer room of his family domicile, appalled at what he was seeing. He'd tried to log into MarsNet news channels, only to discover that none of them were operating. There was simply a warning on each that they had been shut down by order of the Administrator "until the present unrest is over." What *unrest*? A few people wanting to know their jobs were secure? Why shut down the news channels over that?

Unless the Administrator simply didn't want the truth to get out.

Still, closing down the news channels didn't really

stop Jame. His father was the deputy administrator, and had access to plenty of otherwise classified ways of finding out what was going on. Jame wasn't technically allowed to access them, of course, but he'd long ago figured out how to get around his parents' safeguards on all the computer systems. He'd done it mainly to see if he could, and he'd been surprised at how easy it was.

Now he finally had both a use and a need for those skills. He had to know what was happening on the Mars that he loved. It had always been so open and friendly in the past. Why was it suddenly so terrifying?

He logged in to the computer scans, overrode the lockouts, and started to work. First, he accessed his father's information accounts, duplicating them into a secure channel. His father would never know that any information going to him was also going to Jame. He checked through some of the files and his worries intensified.

The Administrator had declared martial law, and sent the shields out to enforce this. That wouldn't have been so bad, except the last ship that came to Mars had brought a whole bunch of new special-unit shields, most of whom were doing the enforcing. Jame knew a lot of the original shields, and knew that they weren't the sort of people who'd hurt another Martian. But the new bunch wasn't as picky. With grim efficiency they were following the orders that they'd been given.

Jame accessed one of the security Monitors, and checked it for any activity. He was shocked to see everything that was going on. Shields were all over Syrtis — and probably the other cities, too. Anyone found in the corridors was either arrested or returned to his or her domicile. In either case, few people made the trip without managing to acquire bruises or worse. These new shields were no better than thugs. How could the Administrator think this was right? What the shields were doing was terrible.

Jame probed further and discovered that most of the original shields had been assigned desk jobs, protecting factories far away so that they weren't near any of the real trouble spots. That couldn't be a coincidence. They were being kept from knowing what was really going on.

But what was the point of all this? Why would the Administrator want to terrorize the very people he was supposed to be protecting and serving? It didn't make any sense at all. Jame desperately wanted to talk with his parents about this, but that was futile. Both of them were working with the Administrator, and they knew what was happening.

They were doing nothing to prevent it.

Jame felt betrayed. How could his parents allow this to happen? Were they afraid of being arrested if they tried to stop it? They didn't act that way. They were worried, true enough, but it wasn't about themselves. It was like they were part of some huge plan, and they were worried about it working. They were willing to let bad things happen to make the plan work. How could they?

He knew he needed to have more information on what was happening and why. There was only one place to get that from, and he hesitated. What he was planning could get him into very serious trouble if he was discovered. He didn't think he would be caught, but he *might* be. Was he prepared to take the risk?

He saw three shields on one of the monitors. They had found an elderly lady feeding the squirrels in Central Park. Her only crime seemed to be that she hadn't heard the curfew warning, and now wasn't moving fast enough to please the shields. One of them knocked her to the ground, and then started kicking her. Tristan couldn't watch any more, but he knew he couldn't just sit by and let such things happen unchallenged. He wasn't sure what he could do about it, but knowing the truth was a good first step.

He had to snake the Administrator's office.

That wouldn't be easy, because there were all sorts of guards against such things. On the other hand, he was good at this. He sent one of his NetSnakes worming through the system. These were really clever inventions of his that could burrow and hide and strike, without being seen. He started the first going toward the Administrator's files, and another to his parents' files. Then he sent a second to the offices, just in case. . . . They couldn't be traced back to him, but each snake would lay an "egg" in the systems. These wouldn't come to life until there was something to report. Then they would duplicate whatever was happening in the files he was checking on, and copy it to him undetected.

He was rather proud of these snakes of his.

While he waited, he remembered a shield officer he'd talked with on one of his visits to the shield offices. His name was Captain Montrose, and Jame had always thought he was a really nice guy. He checked to see where the captain had been assigned, and saw that it was at a desk job in the shield building. Jame patched through a call to him. Maybe he could find something out this way.

"Hi. Jame, isn't it?" the captain asked. "What's wrong?"

"This curfew business," Jame informed him.

"Don't worry about it," the shield said. "It won't be for long. There's just a few hotheads causing trouble, that's all. When they've been arrested, everything will return to normal."

"Why aren't you arresting them?" Jame asked.

"I'm on desk duty right now," Montrose explained.

"So are all the regular shields," Jame informed him. "Only the new special units are out on patrol. And they're beating people up."

"What?" Montrose's eyes narrowed. "How do you know that?"

"I've hacked into the security system," Jame confessed, knowing it could get him into trouble. Right now he didn't care. He needed help. "Aren't you watching it?"

"I was told it was temporarily out of order," the captain answered angrily. "I can't access it."

"No problem." Jame typed into his speedboard for a moment, diverting part of his own flow to the captain's Terminal. "That should free it up for you," he said.

"Thanks." The captain scrolled through what Jame had seen, his face growing more and more disturbed by the second. "This is . . . horrible," he said finally. "Those shields are just plain thugs. I've got to get something done."

"They're acting under the orders of the Administrator," Jame reminded him. "I don't think protesting to your boss will get you very far."

That stopped Montrose dead. "No," he agreed thoughtfully. "No, I don't suppose it would." He thought for a moment. "Okay, Jame. Thanks for your help. You'd better get off this line now. I wouldn't want to get you in trouble." He held up a warning hand. "Stay out of this. I have a suspicion that the worst is yet to come. It looks to me like our chief is trying to seize control of Mars for himself, and it could get very nasty." He cut the connection.

Jame didn't know what the captain planned to do, but he felt a little relieved that *somebody* would be doing something about the horrors out there. He sat at his Terminal, wondering what to do next, when one of his eggs came to life. It was the one in the Administrator's office. There was a message coming in from Earth for him. Maybe some official there wanted him to stop this madness? Jame duplicated the feed, and set it into a small Screen, so he could shut it off and record it in case either of his parents came in. He couldn't let them know what he was doing.

It wasn't what he'd been expecting. On his Screen, he saw both lines. On the left was the Administrator, looking smug and happy. On the right was some kind of *shape,* only vaguely human. It was dark and smoky, and it was impossible to make out details. Because of the time lag in communications to and from Earth, this would be more like a series of talks, one after another, rather than a straight conversation.

"Administrator, I trust you have good news for myself and Quietus?" the shadowy figure demanded. His voice echoed, obviously disguised.

"Yes, Malefactor," the Administrator answered. "The shields we were provided with are working admirably. Martial law has been imposed and my control over affairs here is growing more secure. We've managed to pull the timetable forward without a problem. I estimate that Mars will be under Quietus domination within the week."

Jame felt a chill hearing this. Mars was being betrayed! His father had claimed that Quietus wanted to do things to help people, but that wasn't true. They were just trying to conquer Mars, to make its people captives and slaves, or worse. And his own parents were a part of it! Jame was numb, hardly able to think. He simply sat there and waited for the next part of the message.

"That is good," the Malefactor finally replied. "You are doing well. However, there seems to be a problem with your assistant, Wilson. He has allowed that brat of his to escape, despite every order we've ever given him concerning the child. The boy is here on Earth, and now in prison. I expect you to deal with Wilson severely for this."

"What are you talking about, Malefactor?" asked the Administrator, clearly confused. "The boy is still here. I saw him only hours ago when I talked to Wilson last. He's certainly not been allowed to leave Mars. We've watched over him with extreme seriousness ever since he was sent here for adoption fourteen years ago."

Jame was stunned. He hardly knew what to think, or how to feel. Mom and Dad weren't really his parents? They were just *watching* him for this monstrous Malefactor and Quietus?

He had been some sort of prisoner for all of his life, lied to the whole time.

The Malefactor seemed to be confused and furious at the same time. "That can hardly be possible," he snapped. "The boy was *here*. I've seen him myself, and there is no possibility of doubt. I want you to check in person on what is happening and then report back to me. Immediately!"

Jame realized that the link was about to be broken. Swiftly, hardly even thinking, he sent a NetSnake down the connection toward the Terminal that the Malefactor was using. It had just started on its way when he realized how dumb that was. The connection had actually been broken minutes ago; he was only just seeing it now. So he called the Snake back and buried it in the Administrator's messages. When the Administrator called the Malefactor back to report, the Snake would go with the transmission. . . .

Now, though, Jame knew he would be in serious trouble. The Administrator was on his way over. If he discovered what Jame had been doing, that would be . . . unfortunate. Mostly for Jame. Swiftly, he shut down as much of the Terminal as he could, carefully preserving his links and taps. Then he called up Armageddon 2230 and started to play it, racking up as fast a score as he could. He had to make it look like he'd been playing this for ages. . . .

A moment later, Mom poked her head into the room. "Jame," she called. "The Administrator is here, and he wants to have a brief chat with you. Save the game, will you?"

"Sure, Mom." He obeyed her instructions. "Isn't this a surprise?" he asked, as he went out to meet the biggest traitor on Mars. And the two biggest liars — his own parents . . .

11

Tristan was feeling a lot better after his first conversation with Genia. Most of the pain had faded into dull aches, and he could move his left arm properly again. Only now and then did he wince when he pushed himself too far. But the excitement at what they were accomplishing made the pain fade into the background. He had known that he *had* to escape, but, when he was absolutely honest with himself, he really didn't see how it could be done. Now he was feeling a glimmer of hope.

The desk-comp that Genia's father, Marten, had procured for her wasn't big or powerful, but it was enough for them both. And Genia was every bit as good as she claimed to be. She had a very different approach than Tristan, and where one of them might have a problem, the other seemed to have the solution. To his surprise, they were a pretty good team.

Aside from that, he didn't really like her. Genia seemed to be proud that she was a criminal, and she definitely didn't like anyone outside her immediate family. She fawned all over her father, but ignored Sarai, his new wife. She treated Tristan with polite contempt, working with him but definitely not getting close to him.

Despite that, they made progress. Tristan had to stop to rest. He couldn't remember the last time he'd slept, and he spent "the night" (if that's what it was) out to the world. When he returned to her cell, Genia was still working. Or maybe she'd taken a break herself and had simply woken earlier than he had. Tristan decided not to ask her.

The other prisoners clearly didn't like or trust him, but they were staying out of his way. Genia's father obviously had something to do with that. Marten had somehow set up a black market in the jail, getting the prisoners a few little luxuries that they wanted. In return, they seemed to treat him with respect.

"Hiya, brain boy," Genia greeted him. "Glad to see you're finally up. I need a little help here." She gestured at the Screen. "That Centrus account you set up got us in the shield operations through the back door. I've accessed all of the files on Ice in there, but I can't get them open."

Tristan nodded; a challenge — just what he needed to focus his attention on. She moved out of the seat, and he took her place. "Triple encoded," he said, after a quick look. "It's just a matter of punching holes in it without being seen. My stealth dogs are good at that sort of thing."

"I noticed that, but they snarl at me if I try to get them moving."

"They should." Tristan sent the proper commands and set them loose. "They're smart programs, and recognize who's issuing the command codes."

"You're a pretty good programmer," she admitted with respect. "Look, you want some breakfast or anything? Not that I'm making a habit of fetching you food, you understand."

"I wouldn't expect you to." She was so defensive about even the smallest of nice gestures. "My stomach would be eternally grateful."

"Okay. Just don't break into anything interesting till I get back, okay? I wouldn't want to miss the fun." She left the cell, still trying to act like she wasn't being nice. Tristan shrugged. He couldn't care less how she felt.

There wasn't much he could do until the stealth dogs broke the encryption and got past the shield defenses. Once he had the plans for Ice and the command codes, they'd have the start of an escape plan. Of course, getting out of Ice was the easy part. The hard bit was getting out of Antarctica. . . .

There was movement in the cell door. Tristan turned, expecting it to be Genia. But it wasn't; it was Sarai instead. The woman was staring at him curiously. "Why are you so strong on this crusade of yours, kid?" she asked him. "What's the world done to you except throw you in here to rot? You don't owe them anything."

He shrugged. "I don't expect you to understand this," he told her, "but I'm doing it because it's my duty. I'm the only person with the skill to stop Devon, so I have to do it."

"Why?" she asked him. "Do you think there's a law that says you've got to be all that you can be or something? Why not let the rats go down with their airship?"

"Because I still care what happens to people," Tristan told her. "They'll die if anything happens to the Net."

"Maybe they should. This whole society is way too reliant on computers. It's not healthy, and it's not natural. It would probably be better if the Net were destroyed, and people were forced to live a better way."

"If the Net is destroyed, a lot of people won't live at all. I couldn't have that on my conscience."

Sarai stared at him in amazement, and then shook her head. "You really do believe that garbage, don't you?" she asked. "You really must think you're a hero."

"No," he answered. "I just think we all have abilities and responsibilities to go with them. I'm the only one who can do this, so it's my duty to do it, that's all."

"Strange kid." Sarai glanced around as Genia entered the cell carrying a couple of bowls of steaming oatmeal. "But maybe you could teach this one to develop a conscience. It might do her good."

"No chance of that," Genia vowed. "I'm conscienc-free." She grinned as she handed one bowl and spoon to Tristan. "Maybe I can unchain him from his instead. How's it going?"

Tristan was glad to get away from the argument. He really didn't think he could get either of them to understand why he was the way he was, but he felt he had to try. "We're just about there." Sarai left with a shrug, and Tristan and Genia sat spooning the oatmeal into their mouths. He wasn't that fond of it, but he knew that there would be nothing else available if he didn't eat it.

"We're there," Genia said, as the stealth dogs finally broke through. A schematic showing the layout of Ice sprang up on the screen. They both pushed their bowls away, but Tristan grabbed the speedboard first.

"Let's see what's behind door number one," Tristan suggested with a grin. As he focused on it, the command override codes came up. Genia had a wrist-comp she'd managed to get somehow, and was downloading the data into it as he accessed it. Within five minutes, they had all of the override codes.

They could walk out of here any time they liked now. *If* they had somewhere safe to walk to. Once they had what they needed, Tristan started to check on the other security systems. He whistled. "Here's a nice refinement," he said, gesturing at the screen. "See that delivery system? There's a stockpile of knockout gas that can be triggered from the main gate. It will flood the whole place without any warning."

Genia grinned. "In case of a riot or something," she realized. "Clever. Maybe we could use that, you know." She was thinking furiously. "Okay, how's this? When the next supply aircraft comes, we flood the whole jail with gas. The guards won't have the time to get to gas masks, and they'll all go down. The two of us go up top. When the new prisoners are brought in, we grab the transport, head out to the plane, and take off."

"Not bad," Tristan answered. "Which one of us is actually going to pilot the plane?"

"Ouch." Genia grimaced. "It seemed so promising, too."

"It still does," he said gently. "It gets us one step closer to escape. We can get to the plane, so now all we need to figure out is how to get it away from here. We've probably got plenty of time before that happens."

"And there's one more bug in my idea," Genia said. "If we release the gas, *we* get knocked out, too."

"Oh, that's a simple one to overcome," Tristan replied. "Check out the infirmary. They have personal breathers there, in case someone has a heart attack. We could use those."

Genia grinned at him. "You really are a brain boy. I'm going to filch a couple right now and hide them in my cell. We want to be ready at a moment's notice."

He held out his empty dish. "You want to return the dirty plates while you're at it?"

She took the dish and scowled. "Don't start getting used to this. *You* get to fetch and clean up lunch."

"Fair enough," he agreed. She disappeared again. He finished checking the schematics while she was gone, and had hooked into the whole monitoring system for Ice by the time she returned. She was swinging two of the breathers by their face-plates.

"The latest fashion accessories," she told him. "How's it going?"

"Fine. I'm tied into the monitoring system. Anytime a plane arrives, it'll let us know. So if we can figure out the next stage, we're all set."

"Maybe we can take a break."

"Not a bad idea." He was getting tired from their exertions, but was very pleased with what they had accomplished so far. "But how come you only brought two film-masks? I thought your father would be going with us."

"Him?" Genia snorted. "For one thing, he'd never agree. He's got a cozy life here on Ice. The prisoners and guards respect him. He doesn't have any responsibility, he's got a wife and a very pleasant, large cell to live in. If he returned to the real world, he'd lose all of that." She stopped talking, looking at the wall blankly.

"That's only one thing," Tristan said gently. "What's the other?"

"The other," she said through clenched teeth, "is that he abandoned me before I was born to live or die on the streets of the Underworld. What do I owe him except to abandon him in return?"

Tristan could hear the pain in her voice. "You can be better than that," he suggested. "You don't have to treat people the way that they've treated you."

She sneered at him. "That sounds *so* like you. I'm sure you'd take that dim-witted girlfriend back if she asked you, wouldn't you?"

"She was only doing what she believed in," Tristan said defensively. "If she realizes she was wrong, of course I'd take her back."

"More fool you. She's betrayed you once, she'll betray you again. I can guarantee it. And I won't ever give anybody the chance to abandon me twice."

"You're scared," Tristan realized aloud. "You're afraid to love your father, aren't you, in case he lets you down again?"

"What did you hack into, a PsychNet?" She glared at him. "Don't try analyzing me, brain boy. Freud was disproved decades ago. We have an agreement, not a relationship. Just as soon as I can, I'm cutting loose from you. You're a fool, and you're going to get yourself into trouble again because of it. And I won't be there when you do."

"With friends like you," Tristan said, "who needs enemies? I was just starting to like you, too."

"Don't," she ordered. "Because I sure don't like you. You're just a tool to help me get out of here. I don't owe you, I don't like you, and I don't want to see you once we've broken Devon's kneecaps. You understand?"

"Yes," Tristan said softly. "More than you think."

Genia started to scowl at him again, when the alarm on the desk comp went off. She beat him to it, and called up the plan for Ice. "It looks like we might get a run-through," she said. "I think the supply plane is here. The main doors are opening."

"What?" Tristan leaned forward and saw that she was right. Someone was coming into Ice. "But that's not possible. The perimeter alarm should have sounded when the plane landed, and it hasn't."

"Maybe you're not the hotshot you think you are," Genia guessed. Her fingers were flying over the speedboard. "According to this," she read out, "there's nothing at all on the landing pad, and that's crazy."

"Access the video feed," Tristan ordered. She didn't even argue, but called up the monitor in the entry area.

They both gasped in shock. The picture showed the two security men on duty, down with tazer burns. Six men in white camouflage clothing were entering the building, each carrying heavy-duty tazer rifles.

"That's no supply ship," Genia guessed.

"No." There was a sick fear in the pit of Tristan's stomach. "That's Quietus. They've tracked me down."

"*Us* down," Genia amended. "Don't forget, they want me dead, too. Now what do we do?"

"What we were planning," Tristan decided. "Only earlier than we expected."

"But there's no way out of here!" Genia protested. "Not even a plane we can steal! What are we going to do?"

"They got here somehow," he pointed out. "We'll go out the same way."

"We don't even know what it is!"

He pointed at the tazers. "I know what *that* is. That's our death. We can't stay here."

The monitors tracked the men as they attacked the guards. Some of the shields tried to fight back, but they had been taken totally by surprise, and none of them stood a chance. Each guard was shot down. The white-cloaked men took off their hoods, and started calling: "Tristan! Where are you? We're here to rescue you!"

Genia shot him a suspicious look. "They sound like they know you."

"They're trying to make it look that way," he pointed out. "That way, the investigators will think this was a jailbreak and not a murder. Get your breather on, now. Then release the knockout gas." He grabbed his own film-mask and pulled it over his face. It covered only his mouth and nose, and there was a small oxygen bottle attached. A digital readout showed an hour of oxygen, which he hoped would be plenty.

Genia pulled her own on, checked he was ready, and then released the gas. They both hunched over the Terminal, watching the attackers racing down the corridors toward them. How fast would the gas act? Would it get the killers before they reached this cell? Before they could harm anyone else?

The prisoners had wisely decided to bolt back to their own cells, staying out of the way of the men with tazers. That made things a little simpler. The attackers seemed to know what they were doing, Tristan realized; they were heading directly for his cell.

They didn't know he was with Genia in *her* cell. That undoubtedly saved his life. On Genia's Screen, he saw them fling open the door to his cell and fire into it. They really killed his bed. With a snarl, one of the men turned to the others. "He's not here. Spread out and search for him."

"Typical shield inefficiency," Genia grumbled, her voice muffled by the breather. "This gas of theirs isn't working."

"They never tested it," Tristan told her. "Maybe it's not being released."

"Great. *Now* you tell me."

"All we can do is wait."

"And get shot to death?" Genia asked. "Thanks, brain boy, but I want a better option than that. Maybe we can slow them down a bit."

They could both hear the approaching attackers as they stormed each and every cell they came to. At least they weren't shooting whoever was in the cell without checking first. Tristan didn't want any more deaths to happen because of him. It was only a matter of minutes until the assassins would reach Genia's cell. She grabbed the desk-comp and her wrist-comp and started for the door.

"I'm not waiting," she told him. "Let's at least lead them on a chase." Without much choice, he followed her. They ran down the corridor, away from the attackers, trying not to make a sound. Tristan had a nagging suspicion that this wouldn't help, and then it crystalized. He tapped Genia on the shoulder to get her attention, since he didn't want to yell — even if he could, wearing the oxygen breather.

"This is a dead end," he told her, recalling the map he'd studied. "It doesn't lead anywhere."

"I'm starting to think that God hates me," Genia complained. "Why is all of this happening to me?"

"Because you're a thief?" Tristan suggested. They slowed down, and Genia dived into the closest unclaimed room. There they sat, panting, while she opened the comp to check on the progress of the killers.

They were still moving down the corridors, checking the rooms. "I think they're slowing down," Tristan said.

"That's just wishful thinking," Genia grumbled.

"No, it's not," Tristan said excitedly. "Look at that." The men opened one of the doors, and the woman in the cell was clearly out cold. "There's no way she's just decided to doze off during this. The gas is working!"

There was no doubt about it now. One of the attackers stumbled and fell to his knees. Another leaned against the doorjamb and then slid to the floor. Two of them tried to run and went down in the corridor. The last ones simply keeled over.

"All right!" Genia crowed. "I guess I'm back in God's good books again. Come on." She started out of the cell. Tristan grabbed her arm.

"We're going to have to steal the snow gear off two of them," he told her. "If they needed it to get in, we'll need it to get out."

"Makes sense," she agreed. "Besides, if there's more of these characters standing guard outside, they won't know it's us if we're wrapped up." She led the way to where the attackers had fallen.

It took both of them to strip the protective garments off two of the men. Underneath, the attackers wore shield uniforms, which somehow didn't surprise Tristan. Obviously the shields had a lot of Quietus agents in their ranks. The only shield he was sure was honest was Inspector Shimoda — and she had arrested him. Quickly, he and Genia pulled on the pants, tops, and goggles.

Once they'd suited up, Tristan followed Genia as she

127

led the way back to the guardroom. As it happened, they didn't need to use any of their stolen codes, since the raiders had left all the doors open so that they could retreat when they were done. Only ten minutes later, Tristan and Genia both stood in the entrance chamber of Ice. Tristan tried not to look at the bodies of the dead guards as he went to the main control panel.

"Now what are you doing?" Genia complained.

"Locking down the prison," Tristan said. "When those men wake up, I don't want them to just walk out of here. Or any of the other prisoners, either. They're *criminals*, remember?" He set the doors to lock and changed all of the codes, just in case the enemy shields had the old codes memorized.

"Look, you were framed," Genia said. "Has it occurred to you that some of the others down there were, too?"

"That's not my problem right now," Tristan said uncomfortably. When he was sure the cell block was secure again, he started the exterior Monitors going. He found what he was looking for very quickly. "Here's how the raiders arrived."

It was a hovercraft of some kind. He wasn't really up on transportation, but it was clearly a ground effect vehicle since it had a skirt around the base, no visible wheels, and no wings. It looked like it could hold about ten people, but there was no reason to expect it to be full when it arrived.

"It's about sixty feet away from the building," he guessed. "We should be able to walk it in these environmental suits."

"Let's start walking." Genia moved to the door and then realized that he wasn't following. "*Now* what?"

"I'm recording a message for Inspector Shimoda," Tristan said. "Telling her that Ice has been raided. It'll send automatically in thirty minutes. Plenty of time for us to be gone by then."

"Your conscience is going to get you killed," Genia informed him. "Probably by the bad guys, but maybe by me if you keep this up. Come on!"

"Finished," he assured her. Together they opened the outer door and stepped through it.

The wind almost bowled them over. It was harsh, and probably freezing, though the suit kept that part of it out. It was also driving snow over everything. Even though the hovercraft was only sixty feet from the building, it was invisible in the whiteness. Tristan took the lead, head down, feet planted firmly. He took small steps, struggling to stay upright. Genia fell in beside him, holding on to him so she wouldn't get lost. If they were even ten feet apart, they'd probably never be able to find each other again. Thankfully, her wrist-comp would enable them to find the hovercraft if his sense of direction was out.

It wasn't. It took them ten minutes to cover the short distance, though, and they had to battle for every step. The side of the hovercraft suddenly appeared out of the white freezing hell. They moved along the side, only to find themselves at the engine. Turning around, they went the other way to the door. It was closed and locked. Genia slapped her wrist-comp against it, extended the probes, and triggered the door override. In the howl of the wind, it was impossible to tell if it made any sound, but it opened. They stumbled inside, and she closed the door again.

It was an incredible relief to be out of the endless blizzard. Tristan's whole body ached with the struggle he'd been through. The sound of the wind still roared inside his ears. Genia gestured at the inner door. Tristan understood what she wanted, and opened it for her.

She slid quietly through, looking as though she did this for a living. When she called for him, Tristan realized that they had to be alone on the ship. He stepped through and saw that he was right. It was a smallish cabin, with seats for eight people, but they were alone. Genia removed her headgear, and tossed it onto one of the seats. "Yow! I was starting to get claustrophobic in that." She started peeling off the rest of the suit, so she was back in her normal clothes. Tristan followed her lead.

Then she went to the controls. "Please tell me you know how to drive one of these," she begged.

"Well, I've never actually *done* it," he admitted. "But I've run simulations on the Net."

Genia grinned. "If you think that's the same thing, try kissing a hologram. Right." She slipped into the driver's seat. "Let's see what's what."

Tristan took the seat beside her, and eyed all of the controls. "Don't tell me you know what you're doing," he said. "Because I wouldn't believe you."

"It's a computer," Genia said, gesturing at the controls. "We'll ace this, trust me." She started calling up the information on the Screens. "Dead simple."

"I hope the emphasis there is on the second word and not the first."

"Stop complaining, and make yourself useful." Genia was studying the readings she'd called up. "They had this thing ready for a quick getaway, so everything's set. See if you can call up a nav program, will you? They probably have an autopilot for this thing."

That made sense. He turned to the panels he was at and scrolled down the options. There was indeed a navigator with autopilot. "Got it," he informed her. "Ready to interface. The only question now is where exactly we want to go from here."

"Back to New York, if this thing's got the range," Genia said. "If we're going to track this Devon of yours, we'll need some pretty sophisticated equipment. And that means going back to my old apartment. I've got the best gear a girl can steal, believe me."

"For some strange reason, I do." He tapped in the coordinates for New York, and then queried the fuel reserves. "Good news — this beastie runs on solar energy. As soon as we're clear of the storms, it should be able to run indefinitely."

"Great. Let her go, then."

Tristan sent the final command. With a soft sigh, the craft rose about three feet. The controls showed that the ground effect was established, and then the main motors cut in. The hovercraft started moving toward the ocean. They had done it!

Genia settled back in her chair, grinning happily. "You and I have just made history, brain boy," she told him. "We've made the first-ever escape from Ice."

"That'll get us into the Guinness Net of Records, I'm sure," Tristan replied, matching her smile. "According to the ship, this will take almost twelve hours."

"Good," she said. "Lots of time to get some rest and

then see what else this thing has to offer. I'll bet there's an arsenal of stuff in here. If you're lucky, some of it even nonlethal." She sighed. "I'm feeling real good right now."

Tristan considered things. He realized that he felt the same way. They would be wanted fugitives, of course, once his warning reached Shimoda. But they were out of Ice, unmonitored, and had at least a vague plan in mind.

It was the best shape he'd been in for ages.

12

evon had rapidly become bored with searching for data on Quietus. It was there, sure enough, but it was so *dull* getting at it. He had to peel away layer after layer of safeguards and send his worms in to hack the information. Where was the fun in that? He might as well have spent the day just sitting around. He knew he was an addict to action, and this kind of boring routine wasn't what his soul demanded. He even tried putting everything into a bright visual form, and had his worms burrowing underground beneath castles, chomping on guards and the lot. But still — it wasn't very satisfying. He craved something more exciting.

He had spotted one thing straight away, of course. He wasn't using EarthNet anymore, but LunarNet. Oh, the two were connected, but not too strongly. That was one reason this stupid search was taking so long. It all had to be done the long way. If only Quietus was established on the Moon, it would be so much easier. Lunar-Net had a lot fewer safeguards than EarthNet had and was so much easier to hack into.

Since he didn't have much else to do, Devon started to play around. What, exactly, did LunarNet control? There wasn't anything else to occupy his mind, so he decided to take a peek.

And he discovered a delightful new game.

LunarNet controlled *everything*. The Moon was airless, for one thing. Computers controlled the air supply. Water was found frozen in the bases of deep craters and at the poles. Computers excavated for the ice, melted it, and pumped it to the cities. The Moon kept one face permanently turned toward Earth, which meant it was a two-week-long day followed by a two-week night. During the day, temperatures could rise to 279 degrees Farenheit. At night, they could drop to the same amount below zero. To keep the cities comfortable, they had to be warmed at night and cooled by day. Once again, computers controlled the process.

In other words, life on the Moon was impossible without LunarNet. And that meant whoever controlled the Net also controlled the Moon.

And *that* was a game well worth playing . . .

Chuckling happily to himself, Devon set to work. He had a schematic of Armstrong City taken from the Net, and he started sending out his worms. They looked like they were burrowing through Moon rock, though they were actually working their way through a large number of computer routines. When they turned up bags of "treasure" for him, it was actually command codes for the various systems.

Slowly, his pile of cyber-gold was growing. It was ridiculously simple, as if there had never been any hackers on the Moon before. There were safeguards, of course, but they might as well have thrown up their hands and run away screaming, as he had them do in his simulation. He was just far smarter than the programmers who had started all of this.

It took time, of course, but he didn't mind that. This was fun, seeing how much he could get away with before anyone had the slightest idea what he was doing. He ate and drank in his chair, speedboard in his lap, watching his Screens, tapping the odd command if his worms met any real resistance.

It was pathetically simple. He almost felt sorry for these Lunar idiots. Real Lunatics! Happily, he kept on working. On his Terminal, the ground around Armstrong was as full of holes as the best of cheeses, and his worms were still digging out gold. He was keeping score, and the hidden piles of gold were shrinking, dwindling away to almost nothing. As he worked, of course, it wasn't just Armstrong that was being raided, but the other complexes on the Moon as well. Their secrets were becoming his. Armstrong, however, was the key, since it was the largest of the cities, and the seat of the government.

For the time being, anyway.

This was wonderful practice for him. He could download the Doomsday Virus any time he liked, and it would wipe the memories of all the computers on the Moon. But where would the fun be in that? Everyone would either freeze or suffocate, and watching that would get boring really fast. No, he had something a whole lot more interesting in mind. . . .

Finally, his counter told him that there were no more hidden bags of gold. His worms had collected them all, and they were his now. Whistling happily to himself — a classical piece by the Beatles called "Can't Buy Me Love" — he set about changing all of the command codes. They showed up on his Screen as flitting ghosts, moving to where the bags of gold had once been hidden. Right now, whoever was controlling the system hadn't noticed anything wrong. And they wouldn't, until Devon was ready to strike. He was chuckling to himself as his ghosts slipped into position.

This, again, took time. He had a quick nap, and then ordered up a couple of cheeseburgers, munching while he worked. His ghosts whispered past all the computer defenses, waiting until he gave the command.

Finally, brushing the crumbs off his pants, Devon was ready. There ought to be a fanfare or something, he knew, but he was too psyched to stop and write one now. Instead, he just let out a large howl and typed the command to attack.

His ghosts slithered out of hiding, and into the places where the gold had been. And then they materialized. On-screen, Devon saw them rip the last defenders apart and take their places, standing ready, waiting for his further commands.

This was rich! Right about now, there had to be panic almost all over the Moon. All of the machinery had stopped obeying commands. At least, commands that anyone but Devon typed in . . . Savoring the moment, he called up on his Terminals all the attempts by supervisors to call their bosses, by the bosses to call the governor, and by the governor to talk to anyone. Since Devon had complete control of all of the communications channels, none of them actually got through, of course. He was so amused at their panic that he almost laughed himself out of his chair.

This was better than he'd expected. He was really enjoying himself, watching their bumbling efforts to do anything, even open their doors. Nothing they touched would work, of course. Only he had command now. After a while, he could breathe without hurting his sides laughing, and he started to calm down. They'd been trapped, unable to talk to anyone, for more than an hour now. Even the regular folks on the Moon knew by now that there were problems. Elevators wouldn't work; doors wouldn't open; computers were printing YOU'RE ALL GOING TO DIE . . . VERY, VERY SLOWLY across their Screens. Every Monitor he looked on showed the terrified faces of the people here.

It was delicious. Much better than killing them.

But it was time to get to work. There would be plenty of opportunity to enjoy himself later. He opened a channel to the governor, who was clearly startled when his Terminal suddenly leaped to life after an hour dormant. "Hi there," Devon said, unable to stop grinning. "I'll bet you're wondering what's going on, aren't you? Well, I'm Devon, and you're powerless."

"What do you think you're doing?" the governor yelled. "Stop this at once!"

Devon shook his head. "I don't *think,* I *know* what

I'm doing. I'm taking over this world, that's what. Right now, I have everything in my control, and I mean *everything*. Nobody can even open a door unless I let them."

"You're insane!" the man yelled. "Release our computers!"

"I don't think you're quite getting the point," Devon said, sighing in disappointment. "They're not *your* computers anymore. They're *mine*. And I charge a very high user fee." He grinned. "Go on, ask me how high."

"This is absurd," the governor growled. "I'm not dealing with a child."

"Naughty, naughty," Devon chided him. "That's not a very nice governor, now, is it? If you can't play properly, you're out of the game. So, since you won't play properly . . ." Devon tapped in a command. "I've just shut down the oxygen supply to your office. With that door locked, I figure you've got about an hour before you start gasping like a fish out of water, turn beetroot red, and then die. Then again, you look kind of tough. Maybe you'll last an hour and a half. Either way, I'll have fun pretty soon."

The governor looked around. He couldn't possibly be feeling the effects yet, but he clearly believed Devon's threat. "What do you want?" he finally asked.

"Now you're playing properly!" Devon clapped his hands together happily. "But you don't get your air back just for that. You have to work for it. What I want is to win the game, of course."

"This isn't a game!" the governor croaked. "It's people's lives you're dealing with here!"

"That's what makes the game so much more fun," Devon answered. "Sort of raises the stakes a bit, you might say. So, according to my records, there are 12,265 people on the Moon. Oops, no, an itsy-bitsy baby was born in the hospital ten minutes ago. Awww . . . she's so cute. You want to see her? Anyway, there are 12,266 people on the Moon. So, for 12,266 points — you have to play *real* good."

"You're crazy," the governor said softly, finally looking very, very worried.

Devon shrugged. "Sticks and stones may break my bones, but you've got no way to get them to me." He grinned again. "So call me all the names you like. I'll penalize you for every one I don't like. But, to be sporting, I'll give you a point for every one I haven't heard before. Isn't that sporting of me?"

"You're insane."

"Sorry, I've heard that one. That's 12,267 points you're behind. Want to try for more, or do you want to hear how you can earn all of those points back?"

The man stared at his Screen and licked his lips. He was so scared it was wonderful. Devon decided to lock the man's bathroom door just to make him even more uncomfortable. This was so much fun. "All right," he finally croaked. "What do I have to do?"

"You have to resign immediately," Devon told him. "And appoint me in your place. I'm going to be ruler of the Moon."

"Is that all you want?" the governor asked sarcastically.

"No, it isn't," Devon admitted. "I also want to rule Earth. But I figured I'd try the Moon first, get my hand in, you know? Play with the little planet before taking over the big one."

"You maniac."

"*Bzzt!*" Devon said. "Another one I've heard before. That's another point against you. You're going to have to hurry up, or you'll never win all these points back." He grinned. "Tell you what, let's add a bit of spice to the deal, hey?" He pulled up a picture on both their Screens. "Look at this. Aren't they *cute*?" It was a schoolroom, with about a dozen five- and six-year-old kids. They were all looking very worried, but their teacher had managed to calm them down a bit and had them sitting in a circle, singing songs. "They're off-key, but who minds? They're just so adorable." He tapped in another command. "And I've just shut off their heat. I figure you've got about — oh, two hours till they become adorable little Popsicles."

"You filthy, depraved monster!" the governor howled.

"Still losing points, sunshine," Devon crowed. "So, sit back, gasp for air, and watch those darling little faces turn blue from the cold. And then give me your answer, okay?" He cut the sound on the Monitor and then turned his back on the spluttering, fuming man.

Oh, this was wonderful! The best game he'd come up with yet. And it really didn't matter much whether the governor agreed or not — either way, Devon would enjoy himself tremendously. This was one of those no-lose situations.

Life was fun.

13

Tristan stared around in astonishment. "This is where you live?"

"Yes." Genia seemed amused as she stood on the edge of the old East River, coding the locks of the hovercraft so nobody else could enter it.

"And you wanted to come back?" Tristan was appalled. The area was horrendous. It was all decaying brick and stone, some buildings actually having collapsed. There was an old building that had fallen into the water, the words PIER 17 only just visible in fading paint. There were rotting waterships in the water. In the background was the wreckage of an old suspension bridge.

And above it all stood the *real* world, on pillars of metal that were rammed down into this mess. A real world that, as they had approached, still looked dead. Devon's virus had struck almost a week ago now, but still only partial power had been restored to New York City. It looked like a graveyard, probably because that was exactly what it was. And the Underworld was even worse.

"I guess I'm more sentimental than you thought," Genia said. She turned away from the locked craft. "But, some parts are much nicer than others. I live in the upscale section, of course."

Tristan could tell she was having fun with him, and he supposed he deserved it. He could hardly believe that anyone could live here. He looked at her with fresh respect. "You grew up here?"

"Yes. And if you say anything at all about how you pity me, or how incredible it is that I didn't turn out worse, I promise they'll find your body in the river tomorrow morning. And, trust me, you wouldn't want to be found dead in *that*."

"I'll take your word for it." Tristan wasn't sure what there was in the waters here, but some of the things they'd passed on their way in didn't look much like fish to him. "And I promise you, no compliments."

"Good. You need to be on guard. For one thing, not everyone here is as friendly as me —"

"*That's* hard to believe," he muttered.

Genia ignored him. "And for another, there are *things* down here."

"Things?"

She shrugged. "There's the Tabat, for one. I don't know what it is, but it can rip a man to pieces and eat the juicy parts before you can blink." She grinned. "It's probably an endangered species or something, but if it comes near me I aim to make it an extinct species. If you chose to save the whales or whatever, I'll wish it *bon appétit.*"

Tristan shivered. He could tell she wasn't joking. "So, where do we go from here? Can you tell one pile of bricks from another?"

"Follow me. I have an apartment here." She smiled. "It should have running water, clean clothes — for me, at least, unless you like tight skirts — and some better food than that blasted hovercraft." She started off into the gloom. Tristan followed.

The trip he'd expected to make in twelve hours had ended up taking almost three days. Every time the hovercraft had shown something on radar, they'd been forced to hide. Getting into New York itself had taken a whole day of dodging and disguising their signals. There had been some sort of food aboard the vessel. It had kept them alive, but nothing more. He could still taste it, and the thought of real food again made him salivate. As for a bath . . . heavenly!

He decided to pass on the offer of fresh clothing for now, even though he badly needed it.

The Underworld got worse as they left the shore. There was virtually no light down here, and there had been no maintenance of any kind for decades. Buildings had rotted, and some had collapsed. They had not been cleared, and there was wreckage everywhere, barely visible in the gloom. The place was almost silent; whatever happened over their heads was masked by the floor that had been built to erect the new city on. Not that much would be happening up there without power. Tristan felt like he was walking through a graveyard at night, but with ghosts that were real pressing about him.

Water had pooled on some of the streets, dripping down from above. Without light, it couldn't evaporate. Instead the puddles and lakes spread and stank. Tristan glanced around nervously, but Genia seemed to know where she was going, and he had no intention of losing her.

It was incredible that she'd spent most of her life down here. No flowers, no fresh air, nothing he had always taken for granted. He was starting to understand how she could have turned out the way she had. And, despite her warning, he couldn't help feeling that she should have become a much worse human being than she had.

"Do many people live down here?" he asked.

"No," she said, not looking back at him. "Most of them die down here."

"How could anyone with a heart condemn people to this place?" he wondered.

"Maybe they don't have hearts," Genia suggested. "They never come here. I suppose they manage to convince themselves that it's not so bad, since they never see it. Personally, I'd like to condemn some of them to try to live here."

"So would I," Tristan said. Even he was surprised at the savagery in his voice.

"Whoa!" Genia said. Even in the gloom, he saw the flash of her teeth as she smiled. "Someone's getting a reality check, hey?"

"Nobody should have to live like this," Tristan said with conviction.

"So speaks the privileged elite," mocked Genia. "Too

late for me, brain boy — I've been here all of my life. I'd probably puke if I had to live in suburbia. And they'd expect me to be respectable, too." She shook her head. "And I can't tell a salad fork from a steak fork."

Tristan burned with shame. He had never believed that something like this was possible. Then again, he'd learned an awful lot about his world in the past week or so. Everything he had always believed in and trusted had been turned upside down. Somehow, it seemed only appropriate that he should be walking the streets of the Underworld with a hardened criminal, and knowing that he was a wanted criminal himself.

"Here we are," Genia announced. "Home, sweet home."

Tristan studied the place. It was an old building, mostly stone, with the windows smashed out years back. It looked no better than anywhere else they had passed in their travels here. But Genia seemed to be wanting a response. "It's . . . lovely," he said.

"No, it isn't," she growled. "It's a pile of garbage. At least out here. Come on." She led the way inside, which looked no better. They went up a flight of stairs. Tristan was astonished that the rickety steps didn't collapse under them. On the first floor, though, there was the remains of a faded carpet. Genia held out a hand to make him stop. "If you go any further, you'll get a real bad sunburn. I installed my own security system, and it's very effective."

Tristan could believe her. Down here, you'd need something like that. And somehow a lethal security system was definitely what he would picture as Genia's style.

"Secure," she called out. "Violet eight-eleven. Mark."

"Mark," said a computer voice from the gloom. Lights came up, and he could see across the corridor to a set of double doors.

"Welcome to my home," Genia said, grinning. "Wipe your dirty feet before you come in."

Tristan wasn't sure whether she was joking or not, so he did, to be on the safe side. Once inside the door, he was astonished. The room was quite nicely furnished, and there were cushions and tables all over. "Quite pleasant," he admitted.

"I like it." Genia looked around, satisfied. "Now I aim to have a nice long bath because I really need one. *You* stay out here. If you're good, I'll let you take one, too." Then she paused. "You know, there's something I can't quite put my finger on. . . ."

"What do you mean?" he asked her, puzzled.

"I get the feeling that I'm overlooking something."

Genia stared around the room in confusion. "Something's not right."

"Maybe you mean," a fresh voice drawled, "that it's odd that your security system is still working when most of New York is without power?"

Tristan didn't know what was happening. Genia leaped toward her store of tazers, but a bolt of power stopped her dead. They both turned toward the door to the bathroom. Several thugs with guns had moved out, covering them. Genia winced, but stayed perfectly still. It was quite clear they had been caught. But by whom, and why?

A young woman followed the men out, and Tristan stared at her in shock.

"Maybe it's because I reset it?" suggested Mora. She was dressed in dark, tight-fitting jeans and a dark top. There was a black ribbon in her hair. "Hello, Tristan. Long time no see."

Genia stared from her to Tristan. "You know this . . . witch?" she asked him.

"This is Mora," Tristan finally managed to say. "My girlfriend." He blinked at her. "What are you doing here?"

"*Ex*-girlfriend," Mora corrected him sweetly. "And I'm here because *you* got me sent here. I was condemned to the Underworld because of you." She smiled. "And

I've been *so* looking forward to getting my revenge for that. I've been dreaming about it, and planning just what I'd do to you. And, believe me, it won't be swift." She glanced at Genia. "And I see you didn't waste any time in replacing me."

Genia glared at Tristan. "Boy, you certainly have lousy taste in women, you know that?"

"I'm starting to suspect it," Tristan admitted. His stomach was twisting in knots inside him. He had no idea what was going on, but he imagined that he'd soon find out. Something had changed Mora, and he had a strong suspicion that he'd spent the last half hour walking through it. If she'd been down here since he'd been captured, it must have affected her mind.

"Isn't this nice?" Mora asked, rubbing her hands together happily. "Barker wanted me to ask you a few questions, Genia, and he doesn't mind how painful those questions are. And I get a little bonus thrown in to sweeten the deal." She sighed. "My, aren't we going to have fun?"

"I strongly doubt we will," Genia muttered.

Tristan found he was in complete agreement with that.

14

evon had been having fun. His probes were starting to turn up some information on Quietus, and he was happily downloading what they had to say. Then he noticed there was a figure on one of the Screens who was dancing around, waving his arms, and looking really, really scared. It was a minute before he remembered who the silly fellow was. Then he turned on the audio again.

"Governor," he purred. "Sorry, I was rather distracted. So much to do, so little time. Still, I'm sure you don't want to hear about my problems, do you? How are you feeling?" He glanced at the chrono. "Still got air to breath and dance around in? How surprising."

"All right, damn you," the man gasped, his face red and very unhealthy-looking. "Stop this attack. You win."

"I win?"

"Yes. I'll agree to turn over power to you. Only turn my air back on. I'm dying in here."

Devon shook his head. "You forgot the magic word."

"PLEASE!"

"There, now, did that kill you?" Devon laughed. "Actually, no, it saved your life." He keyed in the command. Fresh air started flowing into the governor's office, and the man whooped it in thankfully. "Now, I don't want you to try any silly tricks. I can send you back to breathing vacuum anytime I choose. So, go about abdicating and naming me the new ruler of the Moon."

"I'm not stupid," the man growled.

"Actually, yes, you are," Devon told him. "That's why I win. But I'm not one to hold a grudge, especially when I win. You'd better get around to writing your resignation, and I'll start work on my acceptance speech. This is going to be so much fun." He frowned. "You know, I do believe we're both forgetting something." He snapped his fingers. "Of course! The kidsicles!" He checked on the class, and saw that they were all huddled together, shivering violently. "Dear me, they look a little distracted. But just to show I'll be a benevolent despot . . ." He turned their heat back on, and then turned their Screen off. It would be no fun watching them recover.

"Right," he said. "Get to it. And don't even think about double-crossing me. If I get even the slightest whiff of trouble, the Moon goes back to being a dead world. You understand me?"

"Yes," the governor said, glaring his hatred through the Screen. "I understand perfectly."

"Jolly good." Devon turned the audio off again, and twisted around in his chair. This was all working out absolutely wonderfully. He was now the ruler of his own little world. If he wanted to, he could kill everybody here without even working up a sweat.

How much nicer could life get?

TO BE CONTINUED IN:

2099

revolution

Enter the *2099 Millennium Watch Sweepstakes!*

100 Grand Prize Winners will be awarded a Millennium Watch!

Official Rules:

1. NO PURCHASE NECESSARY. To enter, complete this official entry coupon or hand print your name, address, birthdate, and telephone number on a 3" x 5" card and mail to: 2099 Millennium Watch Sweepstakes, c/o Scholastic Inc., P.O. Box 7500, Jefferson City, MO 65101. Scholastic is not responsible for late, lost, stolen, misdirected, damaged, or postage-due entries.

2. Sweepstakes open to residents of the USA no older than 16 as of 12/1/00, except employees of Scholastic Inc., its respective affiliates and subsidiaries and their respective advertising, promotion, and fulfillment agencies, and the immediate families of each. Sweepstakes is void where prohibited by law.

3. Winners will be selected at random on or about 2/15/00, by Scholastic Inc., whose decision is final. Odds of winning are dependent on the number of entries received. Except where prohibited, by accepting the prize, winner consents to the use of his/her name, age, entry, and/or likeness by sponsors for publicity purposes without further notice or compensation. Winners will be notified by mail and will be required to sign and return an affidavit of eligibility and liability release within fourteen days of notification, or the prize will be forfeited and awarded to an alternate winner.

4. Grand prize: One hundred grand prize winners will receive a 2099 Millennium Watch (estimated retail value: $25.00).

5. Prize is non-transferable, not returnable, and cannot be sold or redeemed for cash. No substitutions allowed, except by Scholastic in the event of unavailability. All taxes, if any, on prize are the sole responsibility of the winner. By accepting the prize, winner agrees that Scholastic Inc. and its respective officers, directors, agents and employees will have no liability or responsibility for injuries, losses or damages of any kind resulting from the acceptance, possession or use of any prize and they will be held harmless against any claims of liability arising directly or indirectly from the prizes awarded.

6. For a list of winners, send a self-addressed stamped envelope after 2/1/00 to 2099 Millennium Watch Sweepstakes Winners, c/o Scholastic Inc., Trade Marketing Dept., 555 Broadway, New York, NY, 10012.

YES! Enter me in the *2099 Millennium Watch Sweepstakes.*

Name_____Birth date_____

Address_____

City_____State_____Zip_____

SCHOLASTIC

2099/699